Billy Ray & the Good News

Billy Ray & the Good News

Frank Roderus

Thorndike Press • Waterville, Maine

Copyright © 1987 by Frank Roderus

Published in 2004 by arrangement with Frank Roderus.

Thorndike Press® Large Print Christian Fiction.

The tree indicium is a trademark of Thorndike Press.

The text of this Large Print edition is unabridged.
Other aspects of the book may vary from the original edition.

Set in 16 pt. Plantin by Elena Picard.

Printed in the United States on permanent paper.

Library of Congress Cataloging-in-Publication Data

Roderus, Frank, 1942–
    Billy Ray & the good news / Frank Roderus.
        p. cm.
    ISBN 0-7862-6449-7 (lg. print : hc : alk. paper)
    1. Christian converts — Fiction. 2. Miners — Fiction.
    3. Large type books. I. Title: Billy Ray and the good news.
    II. Title.
    PS3568.O346B5 2004
        813'.54—dc22   2004045995

For Howard Deshong,
Pete, and Mabel

As the Founder/CEO of NAVH, the only national health agency solely devoted to those who, although not totally blind, have an eye disease which could lead to serious visual impairment, I am pleased to recognize Thorndike Press* as one of the leading publishers in the large print field.

Founded in 1954 in San Francisco to prepare large print textbooks for partially seeing children, NAVH became the pioneer and standard setting agency in the preparation of large type.

Today, those publishers who meet our standards carry the prestigious "Seal of Approval" indicating high quality large print. We are delighted that Thorndike Press is one of the publishers whose titles meet these standards. We are also pleased to recognize the significant contribution Thorndike Press is making in this important and growing field.

Lorraine H. Marchi, L.H.D.
Founder/CEO
NAVH

* Thorndike Press encompasses the following imprints: Thorndike, Wheeler, Walker and Large Print Press.

Chapter 1

Billy Ray Halstad grinned as he leaned forward to tap an answering note on the signal bell.

Yessir, Saturday night and the crew on Five Level was coming up. Yessir. Saturday night, payday night, end of shift, and hell waiting out there to be raised. Yessir.

Billy Ray was still grinning. He reached over to throw the lever, checked the markings on the cable in the big drum, and threw the clutch off the steam-driven donkey engine. The drum jerked into motion, paying out cable, and more than two thousand feet under Billy Ray's feet the big bucket began to drop.

He kept an eye on the faded, grease-covered red markings on the cable and counted it down. When he knew the bucket was nearing the tunnel entry he eased off on the lever, stopped that rascal within a couple inches of where he wanted it to be, and set the brake on the big drum. He tapped a short ready signal on the bell cord and waited.

There was already so much weight of cable and bucket dangling that he could not tell when the crew was loading, but he knew they were down there. Knew what they were doing. Getting into the ore bucket just as fast as they could manage it, that's what they were doing. And no wonder. This was payday Saturday night, wasn't it. Hell, yes.

Billy Ray had been down there. Once. He wouldn't go down again, but he remembered it well enough. And not just the choking, heavy-chested sensation that told him underground wasn't the place for him. He remembered every minute of that shift. Drillers and muckers and the hoity-toity powder monkeys who thought they were so high class . . . and who got paid like they really were just for handling a little powder and fuse. Billy Ray wasn't worried any by that stuff. It was just that being so damn far underground that got to him, and he didn't have to care about that with the job he'd finally landed after a couple years of working with the crushers and separators.

He could as good as see the boys as they piled into the bucket, all of them dust-covered and filthy, carbide lamps glaring off their caps — that was one thing he hadn't expected when he was down below that time — he had really expected it to be dark down there. But the way the lamps worked, those reflectors put the light right straight out in front of you. So wherever you looked there was light. It might be dark behind you, but you couldn't actually see it to know that it was so, and those lamps made the lighting just fine. He hadn't thought of that until he saw it for himself.

He grinned, knowing the boys coming off shift would be grinning too, them knowing just as good as he did that it was payday Saturday night. They'd be grinning big, and with all the dust and mud and junk on their faces all you'd be able to see of them down there would be lamps and teeth and eyeballs. But nobody'd care because this was payday night, and there was fun to be had.

The shift foreman hit the signal cord and tugged out the message that they were loaded and ready. Billy Ray's grin got bigger. Those boys would want up in a hurry. Well, he'd give them a good ride.

He gave the boys an answer on the bell, then threw in his lever and hit the clutch.

The donkey groaned just damn near like a real live one and hissed some steam, and the drum began to wind in cable for all it was worth. He'd have those boys up to ground level in no time.

He was having fun, but he kept an eye on the cable spool too. Once, just once, he'd brought 'er up a hair too far and like to bounced the whole rig loose when the cable eye on top of that bucket jammed into the big old iron support braces over the shaft. Lucky for him there hadn't been any real damage done or he'd have been out of a job. As it was he'd gotten himself a first-class chewing from the shift foreman and then another to beat it from his own boss. Huh uh. He wasn't having any more of that, thank you.

The cable wound onto the huge spool, the bucket coming up faster and faster as the added cable increased the throw of the pull with every revolution of the spool. Some of those boys were likely getting butterflies in their bellies by now. Billy Ray grinned some more, judged he'd scared them just about as much as he dared, and eased off the lever in time to bring them to a nice, smooth stop at the ground level cage.

"Gennelmen," he called out to them.

"Welcome back to the world."

Most of the boys were so anxious to get down to the pay window that they didn't bother to answer. Tommy Johnson, looking just as dirty and owl-eyed as Billy Ray expected, gave him a wink and a thumbs-up sign as he crawled out of the bucket and stepped across to solid footing. Tommy didn't seem to mind in the slightest that there was near three thousand feet of shaft under his feet when he stepped from the bucket to the landing. Just thinking about that drop made Billy Ray shiver. Billy Ray didn't go a lick closer to the top of that shaft than he had to. He even did his gear oiling from as far away as his arms would allow it. And that was pretty far, him being so long and lanky.

"See you down below," Tommy called to him as he filed down the stairs with the rest of the boys.

"I won't be long," Billy Ray called after him. "Got one more level to bring up."

"Okay."

One more level and then it would be payday. Yessir.

Billy Ray didn't wait for the boys on Three Level to signal for the bucket. He went around and closed the safety gate — some safety; the gate wasn't more than a

11

couple feet high and mostly was there to stop ore carts from rolling into the hole — and let the bucket down to Three, signaling his on-the-way warning after the bucket was already in motion.

No time to waste here. This, in case nobody'd thought of it already, was payday Saturday night.

He had to wait a couple minutes, then somebody down on Three ticked the bell cord to let him know they were there and loading. There wasn't any foreman down there with them, just three fellas on an extra shift doing some cleanup work in one of the old stopes.

There was another short wait and then the signal that they were ready to haul. Billy Ray brought the bucket up hard and fast and stopped it smack at the landing level. A straightedge ruler laid off the edge of the landing would have been perfectly squared on the bucket floor. He was sure of that.

One of the boys hopped out to swing the gate open, and the other two pushed the cart out, having to heave and wiggle it some to line it up with the tracks laid into the floor and leading over to the chute that was the start of the separation process.

From up here at the top of things the shaft ran straight down into the mountain and the plant ran down the outside of the mountain.

It was a right sensible arrangement. Once they got the bulky ore up to the top of the shaft by way of Billy Ray and his steam donkey, everything else was hauled by gravity as the processing went on in steps, each one below the last. Breaking the rock. Crushing it fine. Separating the metals out of the raw ore by floating it on chemicals and skimming the concentrate off with the foam. Finally hauling the shiny, charcoal-colored gunk off in wagons to have it sold for smelting or refinement or whatever else somebody did to it. That wasn't part of the Chagra No. 1's job so Billy Ray didn't know much about that. Or care, for that matter. It was what happened here that put his pay in his pocket.

The boys in the last shift to come up top got the cart on the tracks, and Artie Alphabet — a Bohunk with a last name nobody could remember how to say, much less spell — pretended to drop his lunch pail while he was getting out of the bucket. Artie never cracked a smile while he was doing it. That was a little trick of his. He would go and do the damnedest things, pull the awfullest pranks sometimes, and to look at him he'd be so straight-faced that sometimes you weren't sure if he was joking or doing something by accident. Artie had the bunk four away from Billy Ray's, and Billy Ray liked him.

Artie and the boys trundled the cart over to the chute and dumped it in while Billy Ray set the brake on his drum and got up from the stool where he spent his days. He put his hands on his hips and bent backward some to get a few kinks out, then reached for his lunch pail. No point in waiting for the middle shift operator to show up. Not on a payday night. Billy Ray had a date down at the pay window. And another one in town just as quick as he could get his bath and his clothes changed.

Billy Ray was grinning again as he took the stairs two at a time down to the pay window and the snowshed that connected the mine with the boardinghouse.

Yessir. This was a payday Saturday night and there was some hell to be raised.

Chapter 2

"Aren't you ready yet?" Tommy was ready to go, sitting on the side of his bunk and pretending to be angry but he wasn't; he was smiling. He knew good and well that his best buddy Billy Ray was always the last man in the shift who was able to get down. It was like this every week.

"You just hold your horses, Mr. Johnson. They won't run out of the good stuff before we get there." Billy Ray winked at Tommy. "Besides, the *really* good stuff don't come in bottles and they never run out of that."

That one got an approving chuckle from Tommy. Billy Ray used his palm to slick back his just-washed hair, checked to make sure his shirttail was tucked in, and for the finishing touch splashed a liberal application of bay rum into his hands and rubbed the smell-good onto his cheeks and neck.

"D'you know what you smell like?" Tommy asked.

Billy Ray grinned at him. "Yeah. An' it's better'n what you smell like."

Tommy chuckled again and got to his feet, turning to snatch his jacket from the foot of the bunk and pull it on. It was summer, or so the calendar said, but the nights were always cool up this high and there wasn't any one time of the year when you could swear that you wouldn't have snow. What with the late snows in July and the early ones in August there were times when a fellow had trouble figuring out which snowfall was the last of last season or the first of next winter.

There weren't any mirrors up in the dormitory room of the big boardinghouse where just about everyone from the Chagra No. 1 lived, so Billy Ray had to take it on faith that he looked terrific. Anything Tommy might say, good or bad either one, would have to be taken with more than a grain of salt . . . more like a shakerful of the stuff.

"Finally," Tommy said as Billy Ray pulled his coat on.

"Waitin' on you, bub."

"Then let's go have us some fun."

They headed for the stairs, and Billy Ray waved to Artie Alphabet, who was flopped out on his bunk as usual. Most of the boys had already finished changing and were gone. Artie was older than most of the rest, probably up in his thirties anyway, and read a lot. Which Billy Ray didn't hold against him like a lot of the boys did.

When they got to the bottom of the stairs they turned toward the front. The big dining room with a table long enough to seat a couple dozen men at a time was at the back of the place, handy to the snowshed-covered path that led to the mine and their work. The dining room was empty tonight even though it was suppertime. No suppers served on Saturdays. No point to it. Everybody headed for town as soon as they got cleaned up anyway, so there was no sense in cooking meals that wouldn't be eaten. Not that anybody'd noticed a reduction in the room and board charges when they decided that but still it kind of made sense, Billy Ray agreed. He sure didn't want to waste time here eating boiled beef and cabbage on payday night. There were better things to do with a fella's time than that.

"What d'you think?" Tommy asked as they went out onto the front porch and hit the chill of the night air. "Fried chicken or the free lunch counter?"

"I don't know. What d'you think?"

Tommy grinned at him. "The free lunch is good enough for me."

Billy Ray grinned back. "Let's go do it then."

They trotted down the steep, narrow path toward the town lights in the valley below, eagerness and gravity combining to speed them along. The path was all right now except for being slick with loose gravel. Much of the year, though, it was no fun to take for all the snow that would be piled around it, and sometimes it was impossible. Hard-packed and marked as it got toward the end of the winter, a whiteout blizzard could make it purely dangerous. Two years ago there had been a man not too long up here, a Swede whose name Billy Ray couldn't remember now, who had tried to come back from town after a bit of a drinking session and got himself lost. He was frozen stiff as salt mackerel when they finally found him a couple days later. But this time of year about the worst thing that could happen to a fellow would be to get so drunk that he fell off the path and maybe broke some bones on his fast trip back down toward town.

Without having to discuss it Billy Ray and Tommy turned left as soon as they hit the lone main street of Blue Gorge. There were plenty of drinking places to choose from — most of the places in town could offer a man a drink — but they had come to favor the Ore House. Mostly because it was so handy to Miss Charlotte's place, which was one of those outfits that had a name for it sounding kind of like the name of the saloon but that served a much different purpose.

"You figure to try the wheel tonight?" Tommy asked hopefully. Tommy liked to gamble, at the wheel of fortune or faro or just about anything, but the damnfool always wanted Billy Ray to gamble with him. Claimed he was luckier if Billy Ray had some money on the line too.

"Naw, not tonight. I got better things to spend my money on."

"I keep tellin' you, dammit, it ain't spending. Exactly. You put your money up, Billy Ray, you got a chance to *make* money, not spend it."

"Sure. And when was the last time you came out ahead at one of them games?"

"Aw, not so long ago. And I'd do better if you'd hang in there with me. I know I would."

"Well, we'll see. I'm not making you any promises. But maybe. Just for a little while."

"I feel lucky tonight, Billy Ray. I damn sure do."

"So do I," Billy Ray said. "But not for gambling."

"You know what I heard in the bathroom before you got down? I heard that Miss Charlotte's got some new girls in. You figure to look them over?"

"You better believe I do. I heard the same thing. And from the stamp mill boss, no less. He's in town every night so he oughta know."

"Hays, you mean? He's a married man. What would he know about such stuff?"

"You ever seen that old lady of his? Reckon I'd be paying attention too if I was him."

"You ever think about gettin' married, Billy Ray?"

"Me? Hell, no. I got places to go, Tommy. Sights to see."

Tommy snickered. "Sure. Like that drum that goes round an' round and the inside of four walls up top of a mine shaft."

"No, really. I'll get my chance. I figure to be a rich man one o' these days."

Tommy didn't snicker about that. He snorted and slapped his thigh.

"Really," Billy Ray insisted.

They reached the door of the Ore House

and pushed their way inside through the considerable crowd that had gathered for the evening. The Chagra No. 1 was far from being the only mine on the mountain and it was everybody else's payday too.

Billy Ray saw some familiar faces across the sea of cloth caps and bare heads. He waved a greeting, and he and Tommy headed for the bar. First they each had to buy a beer. Then they would pile into the free lunch spread.

And then . . . why, this was payday Saturday night. There was no telling what a fellow might find to get into on a fine night like this one. And whatever it was, Billy Ray figured to buy into the game. He let out a whoop of sheer exuberance and took hold of Tommy's elbow to pull him all the quicker toward the boys at the bar.

Chapter 3

Billy Ray drained off the last of his beer in one extra long swallow and slammed the empty tin mug down onto the bar. "Refill," he called loudly.

"Make it two," Tommy added, just as loud.

The bartender didn't respond. He was already so busy he needed an extra pair of arms to keep up with the pace of his pouring. Saturday nights were pretty good business for the Ore House. Not that that ever seemed to please the bartender. He was a sour kind of old so-and-so who acted like he wasn't ever pleased with anything anyway, so that didn't matter.

Tommy made sure the man had heard by banging his empty on the bar a couple times. Which was probably why there weren't any glass mugs in the place. They wouldn't have lasted half an hour in this crowd. There were places in town that did serve drinks in proper glasses, but working stiffs like Billy Ray and Tommy wouldn't have been welcome in any of those. Those fancy places were for foremen and supervisors and geologists and the like. Billy Ray had no idea where the really rich guys like the managers and owners went to do their drinking. Or even if people at such unreachable heights did go to saloons. Maybe people like that didn't have to go out to find their fun. They probably spent all their time holding galas in their drawing rooms. Whatever a drawing room was. A name like that conjured up visions of high-toned swells sitting around making pictures of each other. That thought Billy Ray found kind of funny, and he began to laugh out loud. Just a little at first and then harder and then finally so hard that he couldn't stop. Him laughing so hard set Tommy off too. Billy Ray couldn't quit until his belly got to hurting so bad that he had to either quit laughing or breathing, one or the other.

"Where's your money?" the bartender grumped from the other side of the bar. Billy Ray had been so busy laughing that he hadn't noticed that the mugs had been refilled, but they had been. He plonked a nickel onto the bar and made a face at the bartender as the old sourpuss pocketed the money in his apron. The bartender scowled, and that got Billy Ray to laughing again.

"C'mon." Tommy was starting to slur his words a little. Billy Ray was sure that he himself was not, though. *He* was in perfect control. And why not. He'd only had a couple beers or so since they got here.

"C'mon," Tommy repeated. He tugged at Billy Ray's sleeve and led his buddy away from the bar, over toward the gaming tables. Billy Ray went along without protest.

"Le's play some blackjack," Tommy said.

Billy Ray was agreeable. Right now he was agreeable to most anything.

Tommy found them places at a half-moon-shaped table where a dealer in sleeve garters and celluloid eyeshade was building a pile of big old dollar cartwheels in front of him and slapping cards in and out and down and around so fast that it was almost more than Billy Ray could keep up with right now. Huh. It *was* more than Billy Ray could keep up with. That struck him funny, and he began to giggle a little. No one else at the table seemed to mind, including the dealer.

The silly-shaped table had been covered with green felt that had been glued down on top of it. It had some curved lines and little circles painted onto the felt. Most of the boys playing there were putting silver dollars into the circles to make their bets, playing whole dollars at a time. Tommy fished a quarter out of his pocket and put that in his circle. Billy Ray reached deep in his pocket for a nickel. These other boys could play for the big money, but not Billy Ray. Huh uh. He slapped his coin down, and Tommy gave him kind of a funny look.

"You sure you wanta play that?" he asked.

"Hell, yes," Billy Ray insisted. Tommy was probably just — Billy Ray burped — probably just embarrassed by the small bet. Tough. Billy Ray had better things to do than gamble.

"Okay," Tommy said with a shrug.

The dealer whipped cards at all the spots fast as snowflakes in a spring storm. Two down for each of the boys playing the game and one down, one up for himself. The dealer had a queen showing, so he probably had a pretty good hand. Billy Ray concentrated on it to figure that out.

The boys on Billy Ray's right were calling for hits or standing pat or busting. Whatever.

"Hey!"

Billy Ray blinked.

"Do you want a hit or not?" the dealer demanded.

Billy Ray blinked again. It was his turn, and he had forgotten to look at his cards. He turned them up, squinting down and trying to concentrate on what they added up to. It took him a while. He'd forgotten that you weren't supposed to show your cards to anybody else and had his lying there face up. There was a nine and . . . something. He wiggled his finger to call for another card. What the hell, it was only a nickel anyway. No point worrying about it.

The dealer gave him this funny kind of look, about like Tommy had a minute ago, and slapped down the next card. It was a four.

Billy Ray was trying to figure out if that was any good or not when the guy on his right said something like, "Wow," and Billy Ray decided he'd best let things stand where they were. But he didn't get that message from his head to his fingers in time, and he kind of crooked a finger by mistake and the dealer got this big grin on him and slapped out another card before anybody could say anything. That next card was a two. Billy Ray could make out the spots real clear on that one. There

26

weren't so many on a deuce that they swam together so much like the other ones were doing.

The other boys at the table gasped, and the dealer looked like Billy Ray had poked him in the eye with a stick, so that deuce was probably all right. Tommy began thumping Billy Ray on the shoulders.

Tommy was so intent on Billy Ray's cards that he hardly paid any attention when he went bust himself.

Billy Ray still hadn't quite figured out what was going on here, but he sure paid attention when the dealer got all stone-faced and paid him off with a whole big pile of those silver dollars. Billy Ray shook his head and leaned down closer and like to fainted when he saw that instead of putting a nickel out onto the circle like he had thought he did he had up and put out the gold ten dollar eagle that was half of his week's pay.

The dealer'd had his twenty, all right, on a queen and a ten, but Billy Ray had gone and pulled a twenty-one.

"Lordy, Billy Ray, this is your night," Tommy was saying. "But I swear I don't think I ever seen anybody take a hit to a hard nineteen before. Buddy, you are a gamblin' man."

Billy Ray grinned and accepted the congratulations from all the other boys at the table, just like he'd done the whole thing all on purpose.

"Listen," he said when most of the excitement had died down. "I think it's time we got outta here."

"Whatever you say, Billy Ray. This's your night, buddy."

"Yeah, well . . ." Billy Ray swallowed hard, forcing back a green taste that kept trying to climb up into the back of his throat. "What I think we oughta do now is to go over to Miss Charlotte's an' spend some of this free money." He grinned and was conscious of the pull of the muscles in his face when he did that. It felt funny to him. Not funny ha-ha but funny weird. He must have had more beers tonight than he'd thought. "What I think," he said slowly and solemnly, "is that this oughta be my treat." He began to giggle now, but he didn't know why he was doing that. What he did know was that he was having fun tonight. Even for a payday this here night was extra fun, and that was all right. Tommy was probably right, too. This was Billy Ray's night. Couldn't anything go wrong for him tonight. He grinned. Not for anybody who could draw a hit to nineteen and come up twenty-one.

Shee-oot. He was having fun.

He swallowed hard again and said, "I think you better take me over there now, Tommy. Quick." He was feeling like he wanted to throw up, and if he had to do that it would be better to do it outside, maybe while they were on their way over to Miss Charlotte's. Or maybe the cold air outside would help. He hadn't noticed before but this place was awful hot and close feeling. He didn't like it all of a sudden and was glad when Tommy took him by the sleeve and got him out of there.

Chapter 4

"Are you feeling all right now?"

"Yeah." Billy Ray grinned. "Kinda." He wiped his mouth with the back of his hand and made a sour face. "I need a beer, something, to cut the taste. You know?"

"We'll get one here," Tommy promised.

They went inside. Miss Charlotte's was crowded. But sure not fancy. This was a place for the working boys, and most everybody had the same ideas on a Saturday night. The miners, scrubbed and shaved and with their hair slicked down, were practically overflowing the big parlor. "Aw, man!" Billy Ray made another face, this one having nothing to do with the vile taste that was hanging at the top of his throat.

"What?"

"I got me an idea," Billy Ray said. "We got all that free money. Whyn't we go down the line and spend it someplace really nice for a change."

"What's the matter with this?" Tommy seemed genuinely to not understand his friend's sudden reluctance to participate in the usual mass outlet for the miners.

Billy Ray looked at the crowd of eager, loud-talking men — a fellow had to speak loudly here to make himself heard over the general din — and frowned. He was not particularly fastidious, but there were an awful lot of fellows already waiting in line here. The girls who worked here were always in a terrible rush on Saturday nights.

"I was just thinking, you know, someplace where a fella could take his time. Not be rushed. You know."

"Only place like that tonight would be the Silver Garter, maybe, and that's expensive."

"I said I'd treat," Billy Ray persisted.

"You sure?" Tommy sounded pleased, though. Neither he nor Billy Ray had ever been able to afford anything half so fancy and fine as the. Garter, just down in the next block from their usual Saturday haunts.

"I'm sure."

They pushed their way outside through a group of men trying to enter behind them, back out into the cool, clean air of the night. The walk was a short one, but it helped Billy Ray clear his head a little more. He was feeling better now than he had.

"Gosh, man, I never expected anything like this t'night." Tommy sounded excited. That was all right. Billy Ray was too.

They marched right up to the front door of the Silver Garter and knocked. Miss Charlotte's was much busier and much less formal. Coming over here was something special.

The door was opened by a girl — not a working girl unless they dressed awful funny here in black outfits and stiff-starched aprons — who let them inside. Tommy snatched his cap off and held it twisted in his big, work-hardened hands. He looked about as awkward here as Billy Ray felt.

"Yes, gentlemen?"

"We, uh . . ." Tommy stammered to a blushing halt and pointed toward Billy Ray, who finished the sentence for him. "We came to have us some fun."

"Of course." The girl smiled. She didn't seem at all embarrassed by any of it, though she looked years too young to be working in a place like this. She wasn't pretty, particularly, but she had a sort of wholesome look about her — Billy Ray put it down to just because of being so young and so little — that made her look like somebody's little sister. It was disconcerting.

"This way, gentlemen." They followed her to the parlor, mighty impressed that things were done on such a personal scale here.

The parlor was as fancy as a body could hope for. It was somewhat more crowded than they might have expected, though. Apparently Saturday nights were busy even in a swell place like this one.

The men sitting or standing or drinking in the big, fine parlor were familiar to them, of course. There was the graveyard shift foreman from the Chagra No. 1. And a man they knew to be the assay chemist from the Lauder Four. Everybody in the place was better dressed than Tommy and Billy Ray, and most of them were older as well. This was high-toned company.

Tommy got to looking shy, but not Billy Ray. After all, he knew himself to be destined for bigger and better things than just being a working stiff. He elbowed Tommy in the ribs and whispered, "When I get rich this's the way it's gonna be all the time."

"You keep telling me that, but I know

what goes into your pay envelope as good as you do," Tommy said.

"You'll see."

Tommy started to say something, but Billy Ray winked him into silence. A different maid was approaching them, dressed the same way the first one had been but this one carrying a tray with little glasses of liquor on it. She held the tray out toward them silently.

"How much?" Tommy asked skeptically.

"Compliments of the house, sir," she said.

"Yeah?" Tommy gave Billy Ray a broad grin and grabbed two of the glasses off the tray. Billy Ray was more restrained about it. He took just one glass and remembered to thank the girl.

Anyway he knew he was going to have to go light on the drinking for the rest of the night. He'd already gotten himself into trouble once that way and didn't want to repeat that. So he was going to have to be careful, especially since it looked like there would be something of a wait here too. He took a sip of the hard liquor and tried to decide what it was. He couldn't guess. Beer at a nickel a mug was his and Tommy's usual speed.

"Hey, now. This is something, isn't it?"

Tommy was standing there with a glass in each hand, his head swiveling around so on the top of his neck that he looked like a big old bird, trying to take in everything all at the same time. He kept grinning and looked just helplessly happy. Billy Ray felt a little bit embarrassed by Tommy's bumpkin attitude.

Across the room a really pretty girl in a grand gown came into the room and went straight to one of the gentlemen who was waiting. She gave the lucky fellow a big smile and took him by the hand to lead him off.

"Wow. Did you see that? Wow!" Tommy looked like he was in sudden love. And no wonder. A girl as pretty as that, round-cheeked and plump and with her hair all done up fine. Wow, Billy Ray added silently.

A woman came into the room, dressed just as fine as that girl had been, and approached Tommy and Billy Ray. She was smiling just a little, looking more amused than tickled.

"May we help you, gentlemen?"

"Yes, ma'am," Billy Ray said quickly before Tommy could open his mouth and mess things up somehow. "We, uh, well, we wanted to do some business here."

"Of course," the woman said, as if that was just the most natural thing in the world. She didn't once look at the way they were dressed nor turn her nose up at them, which Billy Ray secretly more than half expected her to do. "Our normal fees are five dollars," she said.

Tommy's breath whistled in a quick intake, but Billy Ray never batted an eye. He reached into his pocket and pulled out the handful of coins he had collected at the blackjack table. He shoved them toward her.

"Goodness, dears. You don't pay me. Save that until later."

Billy Ray blushed. He should have known that. Somehow.

"When you select a suitable, um, companion," the woman was saying, "please make your decision known to the young lady in question. We are busy this evening, as you can see, and we do not care to rush our guests. But please make yourselves comfortable. We want you to have an enjoyable experience here." She still seemed awfully amused by something, and Billy Ray could just guess what that something would be. He wasn't leaving, though. This here was special, and he was going to enjoy it right to the hilt.

"If you need anything, please let us know," the woman said.

"Yes'm."

She left them, and this time it was Tommy who dug an elbow into Billy Ray's ribs. Tommy was still grinning.

"Yeah," Billy Ray agreed.

This was living. This was the way a fella ought to have it. This place was classy.

There was a commotion off toward the big staircase that led upstairs. A drunk was coming down, being helped by a patient, really pretty young woman. Billy Ray recognized the man. He was one of the business bigwigs in town. Billy Ray had seen him often enough before, but never like this.

The fellow made it to the bottom of the steps and stumbled. The girl he'd been with had to grab him by the arm to keep him from falling down. That struck Billy Ray funny — maybe he wasn't quite so much over the drinking he'd been doing tonight as he had thought — and he burst out in a loud horselaugh. The man — a Mr. James — heard the laughing and took offense. He clouded over and got all red in the face, got his balance back and stalked over to stand in front of Tommy and Billy Ray.

"What are you two doing here?" he demanded in a loud, drunkard's voice. "Get out. D'you hear me? Get out. Right now." He sounded nasty about it.

Tommy looked worried and tried to back away, but Billy Ray's response was quick anger. The kind that came over him sometimes, even when he hadn't been drinking. And tonight he'd been pretty thoroughly drunk himself and wasn't all that much past it. Billy Ray clouded up to meet Mr. James's fury and balled his big hands into fists. "You got no right to . . ."

Mr. James, who really ought to have known better, if only because Billy Ray was half his age and a good head taller, clenched his soft hands into fists and landed a pretty good wallop onto the front of Billy Ray's chest.

Tommy grabbed for Billy Ray's arm, but by then it was too late.

Billy Ray might not know a whole lot about how a gentleman conducted himself in a fine place like this. But he sure knew what to do if somebody took a poke at him. And backing away wasn't it.

He looped a smack toward Mr. James that would have taken the man's jaw off the front of his face if it had landed, but right now Billy Ray's aim and coordination weren't all they should have been. Mr. James retaliated with a hard punch that bounced off the front of Billy Ray's face. Billy Ray still felt numb enough that that didn't bother him, but the impact woke him up enough that he was willing to get serious about all the fighting this rich fella wanted to do.

He was distantly aware that Tommy was pulling at him, trying to haul him aside, and that somebody across the room was bellowing and sounding awfully angry. But right at that moment Billy Ray didn't care about any of that. Right at that moment he was busy getting to enjoy the fight and seeing what he could do to hold up his end of it.

He was doing pretty well with it, too, until Tommy — or maybe it was somebody else that he didn't see — cracked him over the back of the head. After that he wasn't real sure what was going on. Didn't care a whole hell of a lot either. He just knew that he was doing all right and in a funny kind of way was happy too. This was a pretty good Saturday night.

Chapter 5

Billy Ray felt awful, truly awful, and not knowing where he was made it all the worse. His head felt all swimmy and his cheeks hot, and the inside of his mouth was positively vile. He tried to sit up to figure out where he was, but that made it worse yet. If he moved he was going to throw up again. That was definite. He couldn't move. Didn't dare.

He opened his eyes and tried to decide where he was. There was a roof over him, but there weren't any walls. No, wait a minute. There was a wall right over there. And the thing he was laying all huddled under wasn't a blanket like he'd thought but a rug. He must have crawled onto somebody's porch during the night and pulled their front-stoop rug over himself to try and get warm. Well, he was warm enough now. His cheeks felt hot. And kind of numb at the same time. No idea where Tommy had got to.

Billy Ray worked on that some and kind of remembered that they'd had a fuss sometime last night. After they'd left Miss Charlotte's . . . no it wasn't there . . . it was that fancy place. Sometime after they'd left there and were going . . . He couldn't remember much of it. He could remember another fight. But he couldn't recall right now if it had been Tommy he was fighting with or maybe somebody else. Didn't matter.

He hauled his other eye open and blinked, although it wasn't all that bright. It looked to be about dawn, with the sun not yet up above the mountain peaks that rimmed Blue Gorge. Lordy! Billy Ray felt a rise of bile in his gorge and tried to make out would he rather get it over with and throw up on this man's front porch or hold off and see could he keep from it. Whatever he did he was going to be miserable. He knew that much. He shuddered. The things a fella will do to himself when he's having fun . . .

There was some sound from inside the house he was lying up against. Somebody getting out of bed and hawking and beginning to move around. That settled that, then. Like it or not, Billy Ray was going to have to move off of here or get thrown off the porch. The married men who lived in town weren't necessarily pleasant when they woke up to find some saturated working stiff laying on their front stoops. Fella could get himself hurt that way, and right now Billy Ray wouldn't feel up to fighting back if a chipmunk wanted the space he was occupying.

He rolled over onto his belly and felt his stomach knot up and his whole body protest at the movement. He swallowed real hard, one time right after another, but that wasn't enough. He wiggled on his belly over to the edge of the porch and heaved some. Couldn't bring anything up and couldn't make himself feel better either. Jesus!

Whoever was inside the house was walking around now, and if Billy Ray didn't get off the porch right quick he was going to be in trouble. Maybe get himself arrested and thrown into the root cellar that did duty as a jail. He had been there before and didn't want to go again.

Everything in him was squawking and protesting, but he made himself roll over and wriggle upright until he was sitting on the side of the porch. He was dizzy and disoriented and when he stood up and tried to walk he staggered side to side on legs that acted like they were made in separate pieces with India rubber joints. Couldn't get the damn things to go where he wanted them.

Downhill was the easier way to go, so he went downhill. The boardinghouse would be uphill, but he didn't feel up to tackling that quite yet. Besides, he still didn't know just which hill he was going to have to go up to get there.

What he needed about now was a hair of the dog.

His stomach gurgled acid at the thought of taking anything into it, but that was just too bad. He had to have *some*thing to get his system straightened out again. A beer would be about right. Cut through the taste in his mouth and set him right again.

The more he thought about that the better it sounded. Go down. Get a beer. Get to feeling just fine again.

That was what he needed.

He tripped over something and fell down but didn't know he was doing it until he was already down on one knee, bent over, and feeling even more awful than he had before and staring at the scuffed toe of his shoe and at the ground under it. Hoo-boy. Saturday nights were fun, but Sunday mornings were hell in a handbasket.

He belched a little, and that kind of settled his stomach some. He tried getting up again and made it on the second or third attempt, though he felt nine feet tall and wobbly as a scarecrow in a high wind. Hoo-boy.

Billy Ray grinned to himself a little and set off downhill again. He was trying to veer over to the right, toward the town buildings where he could get that beer he needed, but his wobbles kept carrying him off to the left, which was more of a straight downhill fall than he really wanted to take but which he couldn't seem to do all that much about.

He was down at the low end of the gorge — he could see that now — just on the wrong end of things. The mine and the boardinghouse and all were way the hell and gone at the upper end of the narrow gorge. This down here was the respectable end of Blue Gorge, and Billy Ray hadn't had reason to spend much time down here before.

The Ore House and that beer that Billy Ray needed was a purely impossible distance off at the other end of the long, narrow town that lay down in the bottom of the long, narrow gorge with the shafts and tunnel openings on the mountains to either side. Uphill too although not by such a steep grade. The bottom of the gorge where the creek ran was mostly flat, but at a time like this a fella got to realizing that water does indeed run downhill and so the upstream end of the place was definitely higher than down here on the low side.

Billy Ray shuddered again and did some heavy-duty swallowing. He made a few stabs at walking up the street beside the creek, but his feet kept backing him up and carrying downhill anyway.

He didn't know this end of town, particularly, but he could see a big old tent set up just past where Blue Gorge ran out of buildings, and there were some people heading into it even though it was just breaking dawn.

Probably more stiffs looking for some of that hair of the dog. Which was sounding better and better the more Billy Ray thought about it.

And that big old tent was downhill too. He could reach it, by damn.

He let his feet carry him the way they wanted to go anyhow and joined the men — some women too, he could see now, though he didn't recognize any of them from the cribs or other such places where a stiff was likely to see a woman in a camp like this — who were heading into the tent.

A couple of the men gave him funny kind of looks, and more than one of them wrinkled up their noses and moved aside rather than walk close to him. Billy Ray didn't take offense. He knew they weren't being uppity. Hell, he could smell himself. They didn't have to draw him any pictures. He grinned at them and kept moving right along with them.

He pushed in through the flaps that pretended to be doors at the front of the tent, and there was a kind of hush inside the place, which was a lot more full than he would've thought.

There were a bunch of folks sitting on benches that had been set up in rows inside the tent, and up at the front — back? — of the thing there was this short, stumpy little man in a black suit and white hair, standing there staring at him so that everybody in the place had to turn and stare too.

"Praise God!" the little man shouted, so loud that it hurt Billy Ray's ears.

A bunch of other people shouted it too, and a bunch of them put their hands high in the air and waved them back and forth.

Billy Ray stood there swaying sideways just a little, like a stout tree in a bad storm, and the stumpy man in the black suit came charging down between the benches right smack toward Billy Ray Halstad.

"Oh Jesus," Billy Ray mumbled.

"Praise God," the little man shouted again.

The little man came skittering to a stop right in front of Billy Ray and reached up — had to reach up quite a ways, too, Billy Ray being so much taller than him — and clamped his hands to both sides of Billy Ray's aching head.

"Praise God!" the little man hollered, squeezing tighter against Billy Ray's ears and rocking his head back and forth some.

"Not s' damn loud," Billy Ray started to protest.

But then he looked down into the little man's eyes, and they were wide open and excited and happy and . . . different. Awful different, somehow. Like they were lighted from the inside. And like they could look right straight inside of Billy Ray's head and not *care* what they saw there.

Billy Ray looked down into that stumpy little man's eyes and off toward the crowd that was still staring at him and then back again. He looked hard and deep and swallowed again, this time it having nothing to do with his gorge trying to rise, and without any idea in the world that he was going to do it or want to, he began to cry.

Just broke down and began to bawl like a kid.

He felt his knees getting weaker and with no warning whatsoever his eyes rolled back in his head, and he passed out cold as a dead trout, right there on the damn floor.

Chapter 6

"You been *saved,* son. Washed clean, son. Washed by the blood o' the Lamb."

"Me?" Billy Ray was on the floor. The stocky little preacher was bending over him, grinning like a cat with a mouthful of feathers, and there were probably twenty, thirty other people standing around behind the little preacher-man with big old grins all over them too. The whole crowd seemed to be taking this as an occasion.

"Of course you," the preacher said happily. "What d'you think brought you here? You come here apurpose, son. Come to be washed clean o' all your sins an' your name written in the Lamb's Book o' Life. That's how you come to be here this mornin', son, and that's just what has happened."

If the little man's grin got any bigger, his face was gonna split. Billy Ray was sure of that. He sat up with a little help from the preacher-man and rubbed at the back of his head.

Funny thing about that, though. The da . . . dang thing wasn't aching him any. Which he didn't much realize until he went to rubbing it, *expecting* it to be aching.

His stomach wasn't all riled and roiled either, which was another awful strange thing after the way he'd been feeling just a minute or so ago.

Or had it been longer? He blinked and looked around him some, but he really couldn't tell how long he'd been laying in the sawdust on the floor and all these Christian folks gathered around grinning down at him. Shee . . . oot. This sure wasn't the regular thing for the morning after a payday Saturday night.

Just thinking about some of that, and looking up into all those faces, Billy Ray got kinda embarrassed.

He hoped these folks hadn't much of an idea of what all he'd been up to these past hours.

He took a deep sniff, getting a whiff of himself which all these folks couldn't help but be doing too, and realized that there couldn't be a whole he . . . ck of a lot of doubt about at least some of it.

Not that the preacher-man seemed to mind. The little fellow's grin did get bigger — somehow — and his face hadn't split yet. Daggone. Billy Ray shook his head in disbelief and was amazed all over again that that didn't set off any aches or ferocious wobblies.

Still and all, these folks were sure as shooting wrong if they thought Billy Ray Halstad had come in here to get himself so-called saved. Shee-oot. No way.

"Look," Billy Ray said, accepting a hand back onto his feet again. "You folks got to understand something. You're all too proper to recognize it, I reckon, but me, I'm one of those sinners you been shouting against. You know what I mean?"

The people around him grinned just as big as their preacher-man and bobbed their heads and chuckled and laughed. They sure he . . . ck seemed to be having a good time.

Billy Ray considered getting mad about that. Hey, they were having their fun at his expense, weren't they.

They sure didn't act like that was it, though. They were grinning, sure, and straight at him too. But it was more like they was happy *for* him than like they was laughing at him.

This whole thing was more than Billy Ray could figure out. "Of course you're a sinner, son. We're all sinners here. You don't get t' Heaven, son, by not sinnin'. No human person can do that, see. You get t' Heaven by bein' *forgiven* for all that sinnin'."

"C'mon," Billy Ray said. That sure wasn't the way he'd always figured it. Or heard it told. Whatever. Not that he'd ever spent any time studying on that particular subject. Huh. Not him. And he wasn't going to start now, neither.

"Look," he said. "I thank you. I don't know what all's going on here, but you got this wrong. I just came in here, well, kinda drunk you might say. And I fell down on your floor. And now I'm gonna go have me that beer I been promising myself ever since I woke up." He gave the preacher-man and his crowd a tight smile and waited a second for them to holler.

They didn't.

"I said I'm gettin' the hell out o' here," Billy Ray insisted.

The whole dang bunch of them just kept on standing there and grinning.

"I said . . ."

"We heard you," the preacher-man said happily.

That man sure-Lord was about the happiest little fella Billy Ray had ever come across. These preachers were supposed to be long-faced and sour and all the time worried about stomping out sin, weren't they. This one seemed to have missed the word on that. Billy Ray couldn't figure him out.

"All right then. I'm leaving."

He said it but he stood right there looking back at all of them, waiting for somebody to squawk. He was their prime fish, wasn't he, and fixing to get away?

Nobody said a dang thing to stop him.

Nothing.

All right, he'd just leave then.

He kept on standing where he was.

After a bit some fellow who looked like he ought to be a supervisor at the very least took him by the arm and led him over to a chair right up at the front of the place, and the preacher-man went back — or so Billy Ray guessed — to what he'd been doing before the excitement.

Looking right smack at Billy Ray, still grinning like he had good sense, the preacher-man set off to preaching again.

Billy Ray couldn't know, of course, not having any idea what had gone on before he got there, but he suspected that there was some shift in direction now that they had them a fresh fish in the catch.

"As I was saying, brothers and sisters," the preacher-man said. And then he cut down to it.

Billy Ray thought once again about getting up and leaving. But he was more comfortable than he would have thought on that bare bench. He would rest there just for another few minutes. Then he could go.

And while he was there it would be only the polite and decent thing to listen to what the stumpy little preacher-man was saying.

It was kinda odd, though. Not at all what Billy Ray would have expected. Not how you can't do this and you can't do that and you'll burn in hellfire if you do something else. But about a bunch of happy-sounding stuff. Billy Ray'd never heard any kind of preacher talk like that before. Not that he had so much experience to judge from, but some things you just can't hardly escape entire. So he knew what he was talking about or anyway thought that he did.

But this particular preacher-man kept talking about how it was supposed to be *fun* to not sin. Which didn't hardly make sense when you thought about it except that this little guy made it da . . . ng near believable.

Billy Ray did think about snickering some when the preacher-man got to saying how much of a waste it was to go out drinking on a payday Saturday night — he wasn't looking anywhere near Billy Ray when he said that, but Billy Ray figured it took him some effort to keep his eyes off in another direction right then — because he . . . ck, that was what a fella did on a Saturday night, that and fooling around with the sporting girls, but that wouldn't have been polite, so Billy Ray sat quiet and didn't correct the preacher for his mistakes about what fun was.

That was okay, kind of, but then the preacher-man got to talking about salvation and how a body came to it and how it didn't matter a lick what a body might've done before 'cause none of that counted anymore.

Now that Billy Ray just had to question.

He stood up and lifted a finger, figuring to ask some funny questions and get this preacher fella all discombobulated.

Instead, dang it, his underlip got to quivering and his cheeks got hot and then next thing he knew he was breaking down bawling again, the tears just arolling down his unshaved cheeks.

And he felt *good,* dang it.

Like some kinda weight had been lifted off him and him not even knowing he was carrying one.

He commenced to blubber and bawl, and all those people were looking at him again and crowding around to grab him and hug him and some of them set in to crying too, and danged if it wasn't the weirdest thing Billy Ray Halstad had *ever* seen, done, or known of.

And danged if he wasn't grinning then too.

Chapter 7

"But dang it, Tommy, don't you see? If a drunken carouser like me could be saved, you could too." It was evening. Billy Ray was sitting on the side of his bunk trying to explain his day to Tommy but not having a whole lot of success with that. Tommy kept looking across the aisle toward where Harold Timmerman was trimming his toenails and trying to sober up. Tommy kept winking at Harold and smirking at about every other word Billy Ray was trying to tell him.

It was just that it was such a dang good thing that'd happened to Billy Ray — it made him feel just so dang *good* that he wanted to share it with his friend.

The whole thing, from when he'd first stumbled into that tent through all the things that had happened since then and all he'd been told, right down to the way all those folks had slapped his back and been happy for him and shared their box lunches with him and . . . everything. Just everything.

Billy Ray felt good, dang it. This was a fun thing. He wanted to share it. With Tommy. With Harold. Hell . . . heck . . . with everybody. He was all abubble with the fun of it, much too much so to let it stay bottled up inside where it wouldn't be seen.

"Shit, Billy Ray, you're no more of a drunk than I am. We work all the week long an' just want to have us some fun on a Saturday night. Nothin' wrong with that," Tommy said, almost willing to get serious for a second there.

"But we been doin' wrong, Tommy. All this time we been doin' wrong. Name me a Saturday night since you've known me that we didn't go out an' get drunk an' lay up with hoors and such. You can't come up with a one. Not even the time I caught my finger in the gears and like to pinched it off before I got things shut down. We just wrapped a cloth around the thing and got that much drunker that night so I wouldn't feel how bad it hurt."

Tommy looked over toward Harold and rolled his eyes just a bit, not even caring that Billy Ray could see what he was doing. "Thing is," Tommy said. "The thing is."

He closed his mouth and tried to stifle a burp from last night's leftover beer. "The thing is, you're telling me that we oughta give up having fun on a Saturday night."

"No, dang it. What I'm saying is that there's other things that're *more* fun than getting drunk and going to Miss Charlotte's."

Tommy didn't get it. He snorted out loud and cut his eyes toward Harold. "Anyhow," he said, "I don't know what's supposed to make you holier'n anybody else. Last night everything's nice an' normal. Today you're acting like some kinda holier-than-thou idiot. What the hell's happened to you all of a sudden, Billy Ray?"

He didn't get it at all, and Billy Ray felt sad about that.

Likely Billy Ray wasn't explaining this as good as he ought to. Otherwise Tommy could understand and want to have for himself this same light, free, clean feeling that Billy Ray was having.

And all of that even though Billy Ray still hadn't had time to get down to the washroom for a bath or to change his clothes. He still smelt just as bad right now as he had when he'd walked into that tent. So it was really a pretty exceptional thing that Billy Ray should be feeling himself clean right now, stinking like he did and not shaved or anything. But it was true. It was dang well frustrating that he couldn't figure out how to share this feeling with his best friend. As for how quick it had happened, well, Billy Ray couldn't figure that himself. All he knew was that it was so. It was just plain dang so, and that was all there was to it. He wished he could explain it. But all it seemed he could do was feel it. He wasn't quarreling with it, mind. He just couldn't explain it, that was all. But he could give it another try.

"Look, Tommy. Now you quit making fun an' pay attention to me." He reached forward and took Tommy by the shirt sleeve, trying to bring his attention back here where it belonged.

Incredibly — it like to made Billy Ray fall off the edge of his bunk when it happened — Tommy twisted to face him for practically the first time since they'd started this talk.

Tommy's expression was so nasty — Billy Ray had never seen him look anything close to that mean, even when they were fixing to get into a heckuva fight — that Billy Ray actually recoiled back from the ugliness he saw pulling Tommy's mouth tight and from what all he saw in Tommy Johnson's eyes.

"Leave be, damn you." Tommy fairly hissed that at him. "Just you leave me the hell alone 'bout that crap."

And then Tommy Johnson, who had been Billy Ray's best and closest friend practically since day one when Billy Ray had come to work for the Chagra No. 1, then Tommy Johnson got up and stormed off to the other end of the bunkroom to stand with his back turned to Billy Ray and the set of his shoulders saying that he was ready to swing fists if Billy Ray bothered him again.

Shaking his head and real unsure about what he'd done wrong, Billy Ray gathered up his towel and chunk of lye soap and went downstairs to the washhouse for an overdue cleaning up.

There was stuff going on here that he really didn't understand, but he was sure that if he could just explain it to Tommy in the right way Tommy would understand and want this good feeling for himself.

If only Billy Ray could figure out how to make it all clear to him, that is.

Chapter 8

Billy Ray reached the bottom of the stairs, waved briefly to Dave who was shoveling concentrates out of the dump and into a chute for loading into a wagon that would take them off for refining, and headed for the changing room where the last of the boys up from the day's shift should be getting out of their muck-stiff coveralls and into regular clothes.

He waved too toward Barney the chemist in the odd little office area, cluttered with burners and crucibles, off to the side where the assaying was done to keep a running check on the ore values that were being worked down under. Barney didn't see him wave. Barney was sitting upright and attentive behind his desk, listening to one of the big bosses. Barney was the one sitting behind the desk, but there wasn't any question about which fellow in that room was the one in charge. Mr. Valdura was general manager of the No. 1 and was said to own a big chunk of Chagra Corporation stock.

Mr. Valdura frowned toward Billy Ray, probably because of the unintended interruption, and Billy Ray ducked his head and stepped up his pace a little on toward the changing room.

He hadn't gotten a dozen feet before somebody behind him called out, "You."

Billy Ray stopped where he was and turned around. "Yes, sir?"

"Are you Halstad?"

"Yes, sir." He wouldn't have thought that a bigwig like Mr. Valdura would know his name, much less actually recognize him, but that was who was speaking to him.

"I need to talk to you, Halstad."

"Yes, sir." But he was already speaking to an empty door-frame because Mr. Valdura hadn't waited for an answer, just went back inside the chemist's office.

Billy Ray didn't know what he was supposed to do. Wait where he was. Go in and join Barney and Mr. Valdura. What. He compromised by going to the door of Barney's office and waiting there.

He felt more than a little bit nervous about this, although as far as he knew there was no reason for him to be. He hadn't done anything wrong that he knew about. Certainly nothing had gone wrong with the donkey or the bucket on his shift. Not for an awfully long time now. And if it was a firing kind of thing, that wouldn't be handled by a big boss like Mr. Valdura anyway. There were any number of foremen and supervisors who could've chewed him out if he'd done anything wrong. Which he was positive that he hadn't. Had he? He was sure that he had not.

Mr. Valdura was talking to Barney again. The big man sounded like he wasn't in a particularly good mood, which did nothing to ease Billy Ray's newfound fears. Billy Ray concentrated on staring at a row of black, cast-iron crucibles on a shelf just to the right of Barney's door.

"I don't want any of your college boy advice," Mr. Valdura was saying, too loud for Billy Ray to avoid overhearing. "You just concentrate on the core samples you are given and let me worry about vein width."

"But I just thought . . ."

"I know what you thought, and I'm telling you for the last time that I don't want you to think, dammit. I just want you to run the samples I give you. Man might as well listen to the tommyknockers as to a college boy who's never been underground. If I'd listened to your kind twenty years ago, mister, I wouldn't be where I am today. You got to have a feel for the rock, dammit, and you don't find that in any damn lab report. You find that right here." Mr. Valdura thumped himself on the chest and glared at Barney. Billy Ray was beginning to feel uncomfortable. Embarrassed for Barney as well as being concerned now about whatever it was that Mr. Valdura wanted with him.

"Look. Sir. I know that vein still shows good values. I put that in my report, sir. But it's so narrow that it wouldn't pay to try and work it. Especially there where . . ."

"No more of that talk, I told you. And no more of your dilutions. I am perfectly capable of making the decisions about vein width. Just run your samples as they are delivered to you and let me worry about the rest. Do you think you can do that simple little thing, Craddock?"

"Yes, sir."

Billy Ray tilted his head and squinted, trying to make out the label on a dusty box of crushed ore sample material on another shelf close by. There were an awful lot of those little bitty boxes piled here, there and everywhere in the place, each one of them labeled and numbered and indexed in some fashion that only Barney could figure out. Or would want to, Billy Ray guessed.

Mr. Valdura turned to stomp out of the office and then frowned when he saw Billy Ray standing there. It was like he'd forgotten already that he had told Billy Ray to wait.

"Halstad," he said firmly, like he hadn't forgotten after all though Billy Ray was sure he had.

"Yes, sir?"

"I've been hearing things about you, Halstad."

"Me, sir?"

"You've been bothering employees of this mine," the big boss accused.

"No, sir." Billy Ray tried to protest.

"Don't talk back to me, damn you." Mr. Valdura looked mad now. "I'm having you checked out, Halstad. I want you to know that. If I think you are one of these damned labor sneaks, if you think you're going to agitate for unionization in one of my mines, mister, you should know that I'll have you broken. And I don't just mean banned, mister. I mean I will have . . . you . . . broken. Do you understand that? Well? Do you?"

"Uh . . . yes, sir," Billy Ray sputtered.

"See that you do." Mr. Valdura glared once at Billy Ray and then once again at

Barney before he stalked out of the place.

"Wheew." Billy Ray looked at Barney and rolled his eyes. Barney shrugged back at him. "What was all that about?"

"Aw, he has a bug in his bonnet about re-opening Four Level," Barney said, misunderstanding the question and thinking Billy Ray was asking about Barney's chewing. "Damn vein is rich, I'll admit that, but it's petered down to no more than a couple finger-widths. Time they shoot all that rock and haul it out, they won't have an average pay of fifteen, sixteen bucks to the ton. Which is what I keep trying to tell them, but Mr. Muckymuck won't listen to me. His gut tells him the vein is gonna spread out again." Barney grunted. "Just the champagne and oysters growling in his belly is my guess, but that isn't what he wants to hear."

"I meant that stuff he was telling me," Billy Ray said. "I'm no dang ringer."

"You been telling people that there's better things possible than the way they are now," Barney said. "I heard that about you my own self."

Billy Ray smiled. "I have been, Barney. I have. But it doesn't have anything to do with the dang union. It's got to do with gettin' right with the Lord. Come t' think of it, Barney, I shoulda come around and had this talk with you before. You got a minute? I want to talk to you about this."

Billy Ray found a chair under a pile of books and papers and sample boxes. He removed the junk from the chair and stacked it all neatly on the edge of Barney's already cluttered desk and helped himself to a seat where he could look Barney square in the eyes while he talked to him.

"Have you ever been baptized?" Billy Ray asked as an eager preamble. It still scared him some to look a grown man in the eye and ask him something like that, point-blank and straight out, but the more he did it the easier it got. He was even starting to have fun doing it, though so far he hadn't seemed to accomplish all that much. Yet. He was prepared to work at it until he did, though, and wouldn't *that* be fun.

Barney commenced to look nervous again. He fidgeted and wiggled and looked away. "Uh, Billy, really I don't have time right now . . ."

Billy Ray grinned and did some squirming himself, but his was with happy anticipation instead of nervousness now. "You haven't been, have you? Well listen, Barney, do I have some good news for you . . ."

Chapter 9

"Are you comin' or not?" Tommy's attitude, like his tone of voice, was belligerent. Almost accusing. Still, he was talking. That was something. They hadn't had all that much to say to each other the past couple of days.

"I told you I am. I just gotta get cleaned up, that's all," Billy Ray said.

"I mean are you comin' to the Ore House with me, dammit."

Billy Ray sighed and shook his head. He was looking down toward the scuffed toes of his shoes and not at Tommy. This wasn't so dang easy, it turned out. This was a payday Saturday night, and he was thirsty. A beer would go down awful good on a Saturday night. Surely it wouldn't be wrong . . . He shook his head, at himself not Tommy, and snapped, "No, I ain't going carousing. I've give that up and you ought to too."

"Don't get snippy with me, mister holier-than-anybody. Damn, Billy Ray. A little dunk in the creek, and you'd think it washed all the fun out o' you."

"It ain't like that, as you'd very well know if you'd only set down an' listen to me. Which you're scared to do, Tommy Johnson. An' anyway, I didn't get dunked in the creek. I got baptized in the Holy Spirit, not in water. Brother Greer explained it." Which was perhaps an amplification of the truth but not actually a lie. Brother Greer had mentioned something about it that Billy Ray hadn't understood all that well, but he hadn't really explained it all that much.

Tommy wasn't paying attention. Again. He pointed at Billy Ray with his lip curled like he knew oh-so-much and snorted. "You. Of all people. Chatterin' and yammerin' at us all the damn time lately, and you ain't even saved your own self."

"I am so. I been trying to tell you about it all this week, but you won't listen."

"Don't have to listen," Tommy said. "You just told me yourself you weren't dunked. You gotta be dunked to be saved. Everybody knows that."

"That ain't so, Tommy. Why, Brother Greer said . . ." Billy Ray couldn't remember what Brother Greer had said. Exactly. Certainly not enough to try and explain it to a thickhead like Tommy Johnson. "It just isn't so, that's all."

"Huh. Even I know better'n that, Billy Ray. I got a family, you know. Did have. And when I was a little kid my mama and granma used to all the time be dragging us to meetings. I practically grew up at camp meetings." He paused and chuckled. "In a manner o' speakin' I did grow up late one evenin' at one of them meetings. With a little ol' blond-headed girl that the preachin' hadn't took any better on than it had on me. But anyway, what I was sayin', I practically grew up at those meetings, and what I know an' you don't is that if you ain't been dunked you ain't been saved. And that's all there is to that." He grinned. "So since you ain't really been saved anyway, Billy Ray, whyn't we go on over to the Ore House and see if we can have us some fun."

Billy Ray was beginning to get that deep-set stubborn feeling like he did sometimes. "Nope. I'm not going to that place with you, Tommy."

"Well, Jee . . ."

Billy Ray glared up at him, and his hands knotted quick into bony fists. They had established a long time ago that Billy Ray could whip Tommy when it came down to it, and Tommy changed his mind about what he'd been about to say.

"Sheesh," Tommy said with considerable disgust.

"You go on if you got to," Billy Ray said. "I got things to do without going to that place."

Tommy shook his head and turned away to hurry after some of the other boys who were just leaving on their way down to town.

Billy Ray was left alone in the big bunkhouse except for Artie Alphabet, who was sacked out as usual with a book in his hand. Billy Ray looked around, but there wasn't anyone else in the place.

"Artie?"

"Um?" Artie stuck a dirty thumb — he was shy or something and never got cleaned up until after all the other boys had finished and gone down to town — on the page to mark his place and looked up.

"You read a lot, Artie. Maybe you know about what Tommy was just saying."

"Wha's that, Billy Ray? I wa'n't listening." Artie sometimes got his pronunciations a little bit sideways, like always saying the "t" in listening, but Billy Ray thought he had a pretty good handle on English for somebody that didn't grow up with it.

"About having to be baptized in water to be saved. That's what Tommy was trying to tell me."

"I was babtized in water, Billy Ray. Cat'olic, you know. I don't know about you Lut'erans, though."

Billy Ray thought about trying to explain to Artie that all Protestants weren't Lutherans, then thought better of it. The point was that Artie didn't know anything more about it than Billy Ray did, for all his reading. Billy Ray thanked him and finished tying his shoelaces. "Are you going down to town, Artie? I could wait for you if you are." Billy Ray was beginning to feel a bit lonesome now that Tommy and the rest of the boys had gone off and left him alone in the bunkroom with Artie.

"Naw."

"Yeah. Well. Just thought I'd ask."

"You g'wan, Billy Ray."

"Yeah. I will." Billy Ray was going to have to find Brother Greer and ask him some questions. And not just about how a fella got baptized, neither. There was an awful lot he didn't know yet.

Chapter 10

"What do you mean Brother Greer isn't here? He has to be here. I have to talk to him. When will he be back?"

"He may be back in, oh, three or four months. If then. Greer is only an itinerant tent preacher, you know. He may never come back. How would I know. And please keep your voice down." The storekeeper licked at his lips and glanced past Billy Ray to see if any of his customers were listening. "This camp isn't . . . well . . . you understand. Render unto Caesar and all that. I wouldn't want to offend anyone. And I don't want you coming in here and offending my customers either, young man."

Billy Ray didn't know what to make of this. Last Sunday afternoon this same man, one of the very few townspeople Billy Ray recognized that day, had been slapping him on the back and hugging all over him and shouting gobbledygook that other folks had said were praises. And now here the fellow was acting like he was ashamed to be seen talking with somebody about the Word. Billy Ray honest to Pete hadn't expected this.

"I got to talk to him," Billy Ray insisted in a softer voice. "Or to somebody. Where will there be services tomorrow so I can talk with the preacher there?"

The storekeeper — Billy Ray thought his name was Aitkers or Aker or something close to that — gave Billy Ray a look that said he was being greatly patient with this young nuisance and leaned a little closer. "There won't be any services tomorrow, young man. Not anyplace in town until Greer or somebody like him comes through again. That won't be tomorrow, though. Believe me, my wife would've told me if that was so."

"Yessir," Billy Ray said sadly. "Thank you for your trouble."

"Any time, young man. And remember, any time you need to purchase dry goods . . ."

"Yes, sir. I'll remember." Billy Ray went back out onto the busy, Saturday night street.

There was a little shopping going on

75

down at this end of the gorge, but most of the activity was up at the high end closer to the mines and the saloons and the shady houses. That was where Tommy and the rest of the boys would be. Billy Ray hadn't run into any of them since he came down.

Probably just as well, he thought sourly.

He stuffed his hands down into his trouser pockets and walked down toward the creek. The smell of smoke from supper fires down at this end of town was sharp in his nostrils and reminded him that he hadn't had anything to eat since his box lunch at noon. But he wasn't particularly hungry.

He wanted to *talk* to somebody, dammit. Dang it. Right now he didn't even care about that lapse.

He wanted to talk to Brother Greer again or to some-dang-body who could make all that good, happy feeling come back like it had been last Sunday morning when he felt all washed and cleansed and warm inside and out but mostly in.

He was losing that feeling. Could hardly remember right now what it was like. That worried him. That and a whole lot of other things.

Maybe Tommy'd been right. Maybe he

really hadn't been saved after all, not having been baptized proper. Not knowing enough to know that he wasn't or that he was.

Jesus, he thought, quickly adding, no disrespect intended.

He reached the bare, stony bank of the creek and found a broken chunk of boulder big enough to sit on.

The creek wasn't a pretty thing. Its banks were just pieces of jagged, broken rock, and the water itself was the color of coffee with cream in it, all thick and smelly with chemicals and junk from the mines upstream.

When he closed his eyes, though, and just listened to the run of the water it sounded as pretty as any other creek.

So he sat for a while and just listened to the chuckle and burble of the creek rushing down across the rocks. It was a nice sound, gentle and soothing.

Billy Ray sighed but kept his eyes shut so he couldn't see the gunk in that pretty-sounding water. Gentle and soothing was nice, but it wasn't what he needed right now.

Last Sunday had been gentle and soothing too in a way but a whole lot more than that. The way Brother Greer'd got him all fired up he'd really believed that he was saved. Maybe he was; maybe he wasn't. He wished he had somebody to ask.

Right now nobody in Blue Gorge had anybody to ask if they had questions like Billy Ray did. That was lousy. Even in a Godforsaken camp like this a body ought to have somebody to turn to.

Billy Ray opened his eyes and looked up toward the mountain peaks and right on beyond them. Up into the night sky to where the stars were sitting there cold and distant. And on beyond those too.

Dang place hadn't been Godforsaken last Sunday morning.

Billy Ray didn't care what Tommy Johnson or anybody else said. Blue Gorge hadn't been Godforsaken then.

If it had been, Billy Ray couldn't have felt all that good.

He hadn't been baptized with water? So what?

"So what?" he repeated, this time out loud. "Yeah, God. So what if I ain't been dunked? Does it make all that kinda difference? Is this business of bein' saved just rules and regulations or is it the way Brother Greer was saying last week. Washed clean and saved no matter what you done?

He said it wasn't something a fella earned. He said it was something You was willing to give. Free. So does it make all that much difference that I wasn't dunked?"

There wasn't any answer. Not that Billy Ray could hear.

He sat like that for a bit, staring up toward the sky and thinking.

Then after a little while he started to grin.

He stood up, chuckling louder than the creek was doing, and felt so dang good again that he slapped himself on the thigh and laughed right out loud, alone there by the creek bank.

"I'll show 'em who's saved," he said to himself. "I'll show 'em who's been dunked."

Billy Ray laughed and chuckled and walked down the rocky bank of the creek and on out into the cold, foul-smelling water.

He shivered when the water got up over his knees and wasn't sure he had the nerve to do this. That quick-running water was cold as the proverbial brass monkey's keester.

Fortunately he didn't have to worry about it very long. He took another step toward the middle of the creek, and the sole of his shoe slipped on a slick rock and both legs shot straight out in front of him, causing a whale of a splash and making him just as wet as a body could get.

"Okay?" Billy Ray shouted toward the stars. "Is this good enough a dunking?"

He hadn't been down in the water more than a matter of seconds, but already his teeth were clattering together and he was feeling half drowned and the other half numb. He wished the half that wasn't numb would hurry up and get that way, because this dunking business in a high country stream was no fun at all.

He scrambled over onto his hands and knees, having to buck the current to manage it, and stood, dripping and shivering and grinning.

"Okay," he said. "I been dunked now and can't nobody say otherwise."

He waded out of the creek and began to lope uphill toward the path to the bunkhouse, moving along as brisk as he could but with his legs spraddled as wide as he could keep them because of the feel of the cold, wet cloth of his britches clinging to him. He felt almost warmed by the activity by the time he got to the foot of the path, and he gave out a whoop of delight at how good he was feeling again.

Chapter 11

Tommy Johnson came reeling back to the bunkhouse some time before dawn. His stumbling arrival woke Billy Ray. They looked at each other for a time in the near darkness left by the single small lamp that was kept burning on Saturday nights to help the boys back to their bunks, Billy Ray's eyes sad in the dim light, Tommy's smug, but neither chose to speak. After a little while Billy Ray rolled over and closed his eyes to go back to sleep, and Tommy crawled still dressed into his bed.

Billy Ray woke for the second time well after dawn. Tommy and the rest of the boys who had bothered to come home at all were sleeping. The close air of the bunkhouse was thick with the sounds of snoring and the odors of alcohol and urine and vomit. Billy Ray dressed quickly and in silence and hurried downstairs.

Sunday breakfasts at the boardinghouse

were served late, and Billy Ray did not want to wait. He pulled on his jacket and stepped out into the morning sunshine. The day promised to be fine and fair.

He stood for a while on the stoop at the front of the tall, cheaply built boarding-house to look down over the gorge and the town that was strung along the bottom of it.

In contrast to last night's activities, it was now the downstream or respectable end of the town that showed movement and the smoke of breakfast fires, while the disreputable upper end of the gorge was nearly empty save for a few die-hard drinkers who were making the absolute most of their one, weekly night of hard play.

Billy Ray took the narrow, zigzag path down the mountainside into Blue Gorge. A wagon road had been built down from the bottom level of the Chagra No. 1, but the road had to follow an angle shallow enough to permit draft animals to draw heavy equipment up it to the mine and so reached the floor of the gorge a good half mile downstream from the town and was seldom if ever used by anyone afoot.

He felt good as he walked, fit, better in fact than he could remember on a Sunday morning . . . He tried to work it out just how long it might have been and had to conclude that he could not remember feeling this good on a Sunday morning ever. Certainly not since he had come up to Blue Gorge. The early sunshine was bright and warming, and he had unbuttoned the front of his jacket long before he reached the town level.

A late partier was toiling uphill toward the Marcus K. Billy Ray gave the man a wave and a cheery greeting and got back a puzzled scowl in return.

"Breakfast," Billy Ray ordered at the ramshackle cafe in the business section that divided the two ends of the town. "A big one, I think. Fried eggs an' bacon an' biscuits with gravy." A man at the far end of the big table who was sitting red-eyed and hunched low over a cup of milk-laced coffee began to look somewhat queasy at the thought of food. He hurriedly finished his coffee and left the place before Billy Ray's order could be delivered.

The food tasted good, by dang, and Billy Ray could afford it this week. He still had virtually all of his week's pay except for what he had had to pass back to the boardinghouse, which the Chagra also owned.

He was just finishing his meal when a seedy-looking little man Billy Ray had never seen before came into the cafe, looked around to make sure the waiter was not within earshot, and took a seat next to Billy Ray's.

"Good morning."

The man did not answer until the waiter had come, brought him a cup of coffee, and left again. The fellow kept his eyes down toward the dark, shiny surface of the hot coffee and spoke without once looking in Billy Ray's direction. "You'd be Halstad?"

"Yes. Why?"

"Don't look at me, dammit."

Billy Ray shrugged, realized that the odd little man could not see the gesture, and said, "Whyever not?"

"Dammit, boy, don't argue with me." The man leaned down to blow across the surface of his coffee and then noisily sip from it without lifting the cup from the table. "I hear tell you're, uh, kinda wobbly sometimes."

"Oh, I don't drink anymore," Billy Ray said, forgetting the strange fellow's prejudices and turning his head to look at the man.

The fellow looked pained. "What're you, dense? I'm saying I've heard that you're a Wobbly. Sympathizer anyhow."

Billy Ray didn't say anything. He had no idea what in the world this man was talking about.

"You know," the little man insisted. "One of Bill Haywood's Wobblies."

Billy Ray still hadn't a clue.

"Dammit, boy," sounding really irritated now. "Industrial Workers of the World. Wobblies. Western Federation o' Miners. Dammit. The *union,* boy." The fellow had gotten so irritated by now that he raised his voice, and heads turned on the far side of the room to stare toward the two.

"That's twice this week somebody's made that mistake," Billy Ray said. "Tell you the truth, though, I don't know what you're talking about. I don't know nothing about unions, mister. I'm just a working stiff. Collect my pay come end o' shift Saturday an' pay attention to my work the rest o' the time. What's this stuff all about, anyhow?"

But now that he had attracted attention from the other men in the place the little man seemed disinclined to hang about and educate Billy Ray on the subject of Wobblies and the IWW and WFM and such.

He gave Billy Ray a look of mingled pain and disgust, plunked a nickel onto the table, and hurried out of the cafe, leaving Billy Ray as just one of several people who were left gaping at his receding back.

Billy Ray looked toward the other fellows across the way and gave them a shrug. They were all in the same boat about that ol' boy, it looked like.

He finished up, paid for his meal, and decided to take another walk down by the creek. If he couldn't go to services this morning he could at least go down to where he'd finally gotten himself baptized. Sort of.

Chapter 12

He left the last buildings of Blue Gorge behind and the last of the ugly rock-dump scars behind him as well. Except for being so bare of trees, the mountainsides downstream from the town were probably pretty much the way they were supposed to be because of all the ore bodies being found up toward the head of the gorge. This country must have been really nice once upon a time, Billy Ray thought. Back before the miners came in and changed things around so.

He idled his way down along the creek. That was probably pretty too once upon a time. He tried to imagine the water running clear and clean but couldn't.

Every once in a while he would spot a bit of bark lying on the rocky creek bank or maybe a twig trapped in the rocks when the spring melt quit and the water level went down — there were some times of the year when this little stream was a real rip-roarer and people who had built close beside it had to worry — and he would pick up whatever he thought might float and toss it into the water just to watch it bounce and bob along with the current. He hadn't taken the time to do anything like that since back when he was a little kid and the bits and pieces of wood or bark would be imaginary river steamers or great China clippers. There'd been a time when Billy Ray had thought he would grow up to captain a clipper ship and fight pirates and make his fortune.

That had been a while ago. But he still hadn't given up on the idea that he was destined for something special. How he'd come to be running a steam donkey half a continent away from the nearest China clipper was still something of a mystery to him. Sometimes it just seemed that a fellow went along like a big, dumb old bull with a ring in his nose, without ever a say-so in what happened to him.

Billy Ray sighed and tossed another piece of bark into the yellow-brown water. The great, many-masted clipper bobbed and danced on rough seas, whirled round and round inside an eddy and almost too fast for the eye to follow disappeared into a raging chute of stormy water.

The creek took a bend to the right there and dropped down a stone stairstep as it fought its way down out of the mountains. It dropped fast, not quite steep enough to be a waterfall but close to it, for thirty or forty feet and then took a sharp curve back to the left and out of sight behind a tangled pile of boulders and scraggly brush.

Billy Ray ran down alongside the creek, trying to keep his clipper ship in sight but not having much luck at it because he had to pay attention to the footing or likely take a heckuva tumble. If a fella fell down and broke a leg this far from town he'd best be able to crawl or he might not ever be found. There wouldn't be any other stiffs that Billy Ray knew of who would spend their free time playing along the dang creek like some dang short-pants kid.

Grinning at his own foolishness, Billy Ray reached more or less level ground still without catching up with his clipper ship and broke into a run as he rounded the boulders.

He tripped over something and sprawled face forward onto the stones and gravel of the creek bank, skinning up his hands and elbows and barking his left shin on something.

"Are you all right?"

89

He blinked, startled, and rolled awkwardly over so that he could sit up.

There was a girl sitting on the creek bank, taking the sun without a parasol, with a book spread open in her lap. She looked concerned.

"Uh . . . yes, ma'am. Miss." He felt his cheeks get a bit warm.

The girl — Lordy, he hadn't expected to run into anybody way down here . . . and run into her was what he'd gone and surely done, too — was dressed plain, looked kind of poor, but she was a pretty enough thing for all of that.

No, he amended, it wasn't so much that she was pretty as that . . . he had to think about it some . . . as that she just looked so darn *nice*. That was it, he decided. She just looked so darned nice that she gave the impression of being pretty.

Great big ol' eyes that were still wide with surprise at seeing him and worry for fear that he'd hurt himself when he fell over top of her.

He'd tripped over her legs — limbs — he could see now. It must've hurt her when he came roaring along and kicked her like he did, but she was trying not to show it. Probably didn't want to have him see her rubbing at her lower limbs, which proper girls were supposed to pretend they didn't have, and so was sitting there aching and not able to do anything about it. Billy Ray felt his cheeks getting all the hotter at the thought of that.

"I'm sorry," he stammered.

"Are you sure you're all right?" She still sounded concerned.

"Oh sure. Sure I am." He jumped up onto his feet to show her that he was unhurt and brushed his hands together. That wasn't bright. They were scraped up pretty good from the fall on the gravel, and it hurt to move them much less rub them together. He gave her a smile to show that he was just fine, though, and bent down to wash his hands in the creek. The water was pretty nasty, but at least it was wet and cold and should help.

"I should be asking if you're all right," Billy Ray said. "Did I hurt you when I, uh, tripped over you? I should've been looking where I was going. I know that. And I'm awful sorry. But I wasn't. I was runnin' along chasing this piece of wood that I was pretending was a big ol' ship . . ."

He clamped his jaw shut. Why oh why would he go and tell something like that to a total stranger. And why was he running off at the mouth so?

"I'm sorry," he said again lamely. "I sure seem to be doin' everything wrong today, don't I?"

The girl smiled. He kinda liked the way little crinkle fans appeared at the corners of her eyes when she did that. And when she smiled she really did look kinda pretty.

"You sure have pretty eyes," he said without thinking.

Without thinking? Lordy, he guessed so. He could've bit his dang tongue off.

The girl's expression hardened — and no wonder after he'd gone and said a dumb thing like that — and she looked at him just as cold and dirty as the creek water. "I do not know what you think I am, sir, but . . ."

"Oh golly. I didn't . . . I mean, I'm sorry." Billy Ray felt just miserable. He took in a long, deep breath and then let it out slow, "I sure am having to say that a lot, aren't I?"

She looked at him suspiciously for a moment, then seemed to decide that he really was just as mortified as he sounded.

"I'm sorry," he said again. Dang phrase sounded just as weak every time he said it.

"You don't remember me, do you?" she asked, startling him just about as bad as he must have startled her when he came busting around those boulders and fell over top of her.

"Remember you? No, I surely don't, miss." That was truth enough. He surely didn't.

For some reason that seemed to satisfy her, and she quit looking at him like she was accusing him of something.

Billy Ray thought hard, but he couldn't come up with anything.

It almost had to be from last Sunday, though. She must have been part of the flock that Brother Greer was preaching to when he stumbled into that tent.

It wasn't any wonder he couldn't remember her, that being so. He'd been awful drunk when he got there, and then he got saved and after that everything was confusing.

Still was kinda confusing, for that matter.

Billy Ray found himself on a talking jag again, likely from a combination of confusion and embarrassment. He got to talking about where he'd likely seen her and why he likely didn't remember her. And that got him going on last Sunday morning and Brother Greer and baptisms and not having anybody to ask his questions of and . . .

"I'm talkin' too much, ain't I, miss?"

"No." She smiled at him again, and it made him feel some better. "No, I . . . it's kind of nice to sit and just talk with somebody. This isn't, well . . . you know the kind of town this is."

"Yes'm," he said, knowing all too well what kind of place a mining camp is. Not the kind of town where a girl could be comfortable, that's for sure. Stiffs like Tommy and the boys, Billy Ray too for that matter, were not known for their fine manners or genteel ways.

"What . . . I mean, would it be too forward of me . . . I mean, would you mind if I asked your name, miss?" The plain truth of it was that he was already thinking that he would like to talk to this girl again. Sometime.

She hesitated for just a bit, looking at him real close. Then she smiled. "Hattie," she said. "My name is Hattie Markle."

Billy Ray grinned a little and introduced himself to her as proper as he knew how.

"I'm pleased to know you, Billy Ray."

"My pleasure, Miss Hattie." He felt himself getting a little hot in the cheeks again. There one minute he been chattering at her like a red squirrel in a hickory tree and now they were getting all formal. He ducked his eyes away from hers — hers were kind of green and gray and flecked with touches of gold but a prettier kind of gold than came from any mine around here — and hemmed and hawed a little.

"Yes, Billy Ray?"

"I was thinking if . . . well, if you wanted to talk again sometime . . ." He didn't know quite how to finish that.

She gave him another long, suspicious sort of look, then her expression softened. "I come down here most mornings. To read and be by myself for a little while."

"I never thought about you wanting to be by yourself," he said, "but I should've thought. I'm sorry."

"What I was telling you, Billy Ray, is that I guess I wouldn't mind it all that much if you wanted to talk again. Sometime."

He grinned at her. "Maybe we could do that then, Miss Hattie."

"I can't come every morning, you understand."

"I work most mornings," he said seriously.

"But maybe sometime . . . ?"

"Sure." He grinned some more. "Sometime." He began backing away, his feet moving him upstream now toward the boulders that hid the view of the town and the tailings dumps on the mountainsides up that way.

" 'Bye, Billy Ray."

" 'Bye, Miss Hattie." He walked backward all the way to the boulders, gave Hattie a weak wave and finally turned around so that he could see where he was going and maybe wouldn't fall down again.

On his way back to town Billy Ray wasn't thinking about clipper ships or river steamers anymore.

Chapter 13

"I need a Bible," he told the man behind the counter.

"I got one of those, I think. Give me a minute." The fellow went off to a dark corner of the store and began to rummage through boxes of used books. Which was the kind of place this was. Used stuff of nearly any description. The fellow not only sold used stuff, he bought it too, as a good many of the boys were aware and took advantage of when they got tight between paydays or were laid up and couldn't work for a while or managed to lose all their pay before they got around to paying their board or whatever. Of course merchandise of whatever sort always looked real different to the fellow depending on whether the customer was buying or selling. Buying, the old used junk would be valuable and dear. But when a stiff was selling something it was always stuff that couldn't possibly be of interest to anybody this side of St. Louis and the proprietor would agree to take it off their hands only as a personal favor. Sure.

Anyway, the fellow poked through this box and that one for a time. He straightened once, holding a battered book with a maroon cloth cover and frowning at it.

"Did you find one?" Billy Ray asked.

The man ignored that question and asked one of his own. "You wouldn't want a volume of Robert Burns, would you?"

Billy Ray guessed that poetry wasn't exactly a big seller in Blue Gorge. He ignored the storekeeper's question just like the man had ignored his, and after a bit the fellow went back to rooting in the boxes of books.

"Ha!" the fellow said finally. He stood up holding a black-bound book for Billy Ray's inspection. "This what you're looking for?"

Billy Ray took the Bible and examined it. It had seen some rough wear somewhere along the line, and pages were missing here and there, particularly toward the back. There was an inscription inside the front in fading, purplish ink saying the Bible had been given to Dennis, Beloved Son, by Mother. It was dated thirty-odd years back, and there was no telling who Dennis was or how his Bible had come to wind up here.

"There's some pages missing," Billy Ray said.

"What's there is still good, though. Regular price on that should be a dollar. I'll knock that down to fifty cents to make up for the missing parts."

"Twenty-five cents," Billy Ray countered, wondering after he said it if it would be considered wrong to haggle over the price of a Bible.

The storekeeper frowned and twisted his face around some, one new expression as sour as the last one had been. Finally he nodded. "Twenty-five."

Billy Ray paid the man and left.

If he didn't have Brother Greer handy to talk to, why, he'd just go right straight to the source of the matter with his questions.

Though the truth was that he wasn't all that grand a reader. But likely some practice would improve on that. And it wasn't that he *couldn't* read. Just that he hadn't had all that much call for it lately.

He would make out.

He tucked his and Dennis's Bible under his arm and hiked back up toward the bunkhouse, where they ought to be serving Sunday dinner by now.

On the way, though, he wasn't thinking so much about the Bible he was carrying as about what a nice girl Miss Hattie was and how pretty her eyes were when she smiled.

Chapter 14

"What's this word, Artie?" Billy Ray spelled it for him, slow and clear.

Artie had to think about it for a bit, visualizing the spelling in his head until the word came together for him. "Privily," Artie said finally. "Somethin' like that."

"What's it mean?" Billy Ray asked the question, but he had come to a low pass, asking a Bohunk like Artie about a word in English.

"I do not know, Billy Ray. I know what a privy is, but I think that is spelled different."

"Yeah. Me too." Billy Ray leaned closer to the open book, as if that would get him closer to the meaning of what he was reading, and tried again to get a handle on the stuff.

"What you are reading, Billy Ray?"

"Proverbs. Seemed like a good place to start when you're lookin' for advice. You know?"

"Oh yes. Proverbs. You read Psalms too?" For some reason Artie pronounced the p in Psalms. "I like Psalms."

"I figure to get to them pretty soon," Billy Ray said. If he ever managed to get through Proverbs, that is. This was tough going and he hadn't hardly got a good start.

Still, this stuff in Proverbs looked to be pretty straight talk, what he could make out of it. Why, already the Proverbs were telling him to watch out for the boys who were trying to get him to forget about being saved and go back to raising hell on payday Saturday nights. Right there it was. "My son, if sinners entice thee, consent thou not." Now that was clear enough.

Billy Ray looked around, intending to give ol' Tommy Johnson a look or two, but Tommy wasn't in the bunkroom. Billy Ray and Artie and a couple boys rolling dice down at the other end of the room were the only ones in sight.

Billy Ray gave some more thought to that word privily . . . it had something to do with lurking, said that right there in Proverbs . . . but he couldn't quite figure it out.

He decided he'd just let it set in his brain for a bit and sat up. He closed the Bible carefully and bent down to lay it on the floor under the head of his bunk, between the wall and his Sunday shoes where it wouldn't get stepped on or knocked around or otherwise abused. The boys in this bunkhouse were good about not swiping things, but sometimes they made themselves pretty free with another fella's things and Billy Ray didn't want anything to happen to his Bible. Billy Ray stood and hid a yawn behind the back of his hand.

Down at the other end of the long room Duane Hunter, who was probably the best singlejack man on the mountain, came up the stairs and flopped face down onto his bunk. Somebody'd turned the slats underneath Duane's mattress so that they were just barely holding in place, and when he hit the bunk he kept on going right down to the floor, which seemed to startle him pretty good although it didn't hurt him any.

Duane jumped up and began fussing at C. J. Tilton, who was one of the boys playing at the dice down at that end of the room, accusing C.J. of having done the trick, which C.J. denied. They like to got into a scrap over it, but Duane backed off, not having any proof of the matter, and things settled down.

As a matter of fact, Artie had been down at that end of the room when Billy Ray came up after supper. So Billy Ray had a few suspicions of his own. Artie never once looked down in that direction and a body wouldn't have thought he was even aware of what had happened to Duane or that Duane and C.J. were discussing it after. Artie never cracked a smile, but Billy Ray thought he saw Artie's belly flutter so he might have been doing some laughing inside.

Billy Ray yawned again and ambled down to the front porch where the rest of the boys, those that hadn't gone into town to get rid of whatever they had left from their pay, would be sitting and smoking. There was a rule about that. No smoking in the bunkroom. The company didn't want their bunkhouse burnt down by some half-drunk stiff without sense enough to put a cigar out. Since Billy Ray didn't smoke he didn't mind the rule, though some of the boys complained about it pretty regular. There were times, like whenever he took a close look at the floor, that Billy Ray wished the company would pass a rule against chewing in the bunkroom too.

Billy Ray found an empty place on the

edge of the stoop and sat down with his legs dangling over the side. "Where's Tommy?"

"Over to the supervisor's office," Brian F. said. Brian had the unfortunate last name of Fartle, but no one ever teased him about it more than once. Brian wasn't all that big, but he had an awful short fuse and even the bigger, rougher stiffs found that they got tired of having to whip him every night after supper. Which they would surely have to do until they agreed with Brian that a man's family name wasn't fit reason for laughter.

"Something going on over there?"

Brian pulled a pipe out of his pocket and began loading it with a coarse, dark tobacco that smelled bad even before it was set afire. "Something about making up a new crew to go back onto Four Level," he said while he studied to make sure that the tobacco was tamped in just exactly right. It always amazed Billy Ray how much careful attention a man had to devote to a pipe of tobacco.

"Oh yeah." Billy Ray remembered now that Mr. Valdura had been saying something about that the other day.

"You won't be finding me back down on Four." Brian went on. "They asked me, but I told 'em I'd quit before I went back down on that one."

"How come?"

"I worked Four before, you know."

"So?"

"Tommyknockers," Brian said darkly. "I heard them, Billy Ray. I heard 'em tapping, and I could feel the cold of it running all up an' down my back. I heard 'em, and I won't go back. Not to Four. Never again."

There were those who said that the tommyknockers were just a silly superstition dreamed up by sillier stiffs who were inventing things to worry about. That might even have been so, but Billy Ray had noticed over the years that the folks who said the tommyknockers were nonsense were all fellas who worked above ground.

You wouldn't find a boy from underground talking any way about the tommyknockers than respectful.

You didn't see the tommyknockers. You heard them. They lived — or whatever they did — in the cold heart of the solid rock, and when there was fixing to be trouble the tommyknockers would come and tap out a warning for the boys to get out.

They made a sound like little bitty ham-

106

mers tapping on the stone, and they sounded out their warnings without words. Just with those light little hammer blows.

There were those — supervisors and the like — who claimed that all the boys were hearing was the settling of the shoring timbers and the groaning of the rock itself. But the boys who worked underground knew better.

Those boys didn't joke about the tommyknockers. Not even when they were off shift and safe above ground, they wouldn't.

Wouldn't let anybody else joke about them neither if they could help it.

It was said that the tommyknockers had saved an awful lot of stiffs. Warned them about tunnels collapsing before anything ever gave way and such as that.

It was said too that the boys who'd got themselves convinced otherwise and failed to listen to the tommyknockers, those boys never got themselves another warning, and a lot of them found themselves dead and buried in the same tunnels they'd been working when the tommyknockers left them.

So if Brian F. wanted to refuse work on Four Level because of the tommyknockers, well, Billy Ray wasn't going to tell him different. Billy Ray was so scared of all that weight above him in the tunnels that he couldn't work underground at all, which he'd sure found out that one time he went down, so he hadn't any right to tell Brian F. anything about tommyknockers. Huh uh.

"Bad joss," Brian F. mumbled, still thinking about Four Level and the warning he'd gotten down there.

Still, a warning for one stiff wasn't the same as a warning for all, and there would be enough boys who hadn't got a warning and would work Four Level the same as any other.

"I'll have to check tomorra and make sure I can find my cable mark for Four again," Billy Ray mused out loud.

"If you never find it, it'll be all right with me," Brian said.

"Lot o' grease on the cable," Billy Ray said, talking mostly to himself as Brian still seemed concerned with his tommy-knockers. "Haven't had cause to mess with Four much."

Billy Ray was really occupied with fears of his own at the moment, although Brian probably wouldn't recognize that.

The thing was, Billy Ray just absolutely hated to have to clean cable or repaint his depth marks. It was bad enough oiling, and that he could do at arm's length with the long-spouted oilcan. But when he cleaned cable he had to be right there next to the dang mouth of the deep shaft, and even if he had the bucket positioned at the top so that it would be hard to fall in even if he fell, why, he got so weak-kneed and trembly that he was apt to take a tumble for no reason. And in order to get to his mark for Four Level the dang bucket would have to be at Four Level. And there wasn't any such thing as a gate or rail or safety strap big enough or stout enough to make Billy Ray forget just how far down it was to the bottom of the dang shaft.

He shuddered some just from thinking about it, him worrying about the shaft and Brian worrying about his tommyknockers.

After a bit Billy Ray quit thinking about it and went back upstairs to tackle Proverbs one more time.

Chapter 15

Billy Ray gave the boiled and starched shirt a critical inspection before he shook it out and put it on. It felt scratchy and a little stiff, but that was all right. It made him feel dressed up and kind of dandy for a change.

Tommy Johnson, who looked plenty the worse for wear after last night, snickered and let out a low whistle, not loud enough to wake the other boys who were still sleeping. Though the usual Sunday morning condition meant that they probably couldn't have been wakened by anything short of an eight ounce powder charge set down right next to their ears.

"Fa-an-cy," Tommy said.

Billy Ray didn't say anything. He was busy trying to fix a brand new paper collar to the shirt and to get something resembling a bow tied into the rest of the fixings he'd bought last evening.

It was true enough, though, by golly. He

likely did look mighty nice, which was why he'd gone to all this trouble, after all. Like having his good shirt sent out to get it washed and starched instead of just wringing it out himself down in the washroom like he used to once in a great while.

All in all Billy Ray was feeling pretty well pleased. The lady at the laundry had sewed on a button for him that had been missing for the better part of a year and had repaired that place at the back of the neck where the shirt had begun to fray. So he was turned out right well here and feeling pleased with himself.

Tommy sat up on his bunk — slow and careful to keep down the pounding in his head — and kind of smirked toward Billy Ray. "Goin' to services, eh?" He made it sound like there was something wrong about going to services. Billy Ray had noticed that Tommy was feeling mighty big for his britches lately. Ever since he got moved to the Four Level crew and promoted from being a common mucker to spinning the drill for Alex Zorbe, who was almost as good a singlejack man as Duane Hunter and who therefore was fairly unlikely to miss the drill and take off a part of Tommy's hand with the single jack. Tommy had gotten a pay raise with the new job and was acting awfully pert since.

"You know as good as I do that there's no services here," Billy Ray said. Tommy ought to know that. Billy Ray had complained about it often enough lately.

"Huh," Tommy said with a snort. "I don't know why you'd say a thing like that. You hold 'em up here 'most every damn evening, reading out loud to us when we don't wanta hear. You better watch that, Billy Ray. Some o' the boys are starting to get pissed about it. I'm only saying that to be friendly, mind. I thought you oughta know. Some of the boys are really getting pissed."

And you right up there at the head of the pack, Billy Ray thought to himself. It grieved him that he'd gone and gotten saved but poor dumb Tommy hadn't. When a fellow came into such good fortune he just naturally wanted to share it with his best friend, but Tommy couldn't seem to see it that way. The truth now was that Billy Ray wasn't so completely sure anymore that he should still be thinking about Tommy as being a best friend. They weren't so awful close anymore and tended to make digs at one another when they did talk, which wasn't near so often as it used to be.

Billy Ray finally got his tie pulled into a shape that more or less resembled a bow. He checked it out in a piece of mirror that he kept in his trunk lately. He worked his mouth back and forth and looked under his neck, checking to make sure that he'd got himself a close enough shave and that there weren't any stray hairs sticking out someplace that he hadn't reached. Then he pronounced himself satisfied.

"Where are you going?" Tommy asked.

Billy Ray pretended he hadn't heard. He didn't want to lie about it but he didn't want to tell Tommy about Miss Hattie either. If he did that all he'd hear in the bunkhouse from now on would be teasing.

"All right, damn you," Tommy grumped. He flopped back down onto his bunk in a sulk. Billy Ray pretended not to have heard that too.

Billy Ray brushed off the front of his trousers and rubbed the toes of his Sunday shoes over the backs of his calves and headed down the stairs, going faster and faster with anticipation as he went.

This whole week long he'd been thinking about Miss Hattie. Even when he was trying to read his Bible he'd find his mind wandering off and Miss Hattie Markle's countenance there on the page instead of whatever prophet or apostle he'd been trying to read about.

Billy Ray Halstad had known a lot of girls in his time, but none of them had been the kind to actually think about except in bad ways that he wouldn't feel right about anymore. Miss Hattie was different. She was nice. And pretty too in her own kind of way. And he'd really enjoyed sitting and talking with her. That was something he had never in his whole life done before, sit and really talk with a young lady. It had been a new experience, and he'd liked it. This morning he sure figured to do it some more.

He practically ran down the steep, twisty path to town. He had everything all planned out. Had been kind of working on the plan for the better part of the past week.

He stopped first at the cafe, as it was early and most of the stores hadn't opened yet, and put in his order, then went down the street to a mercantile that always opened early on Sunday mornings and sold a lot of patent medicines and other guaranteed cures for the stiffs who were still liquor-stiff from the night before. Billy Ray didn't need any of the coca pick-me-ups, though. Not today, he didn't. He knew just what he wanted and went straight to the things. He bought a cunning little wicker basket and a swatch of clean cloth about a yard square and two real linen napkins and two each of butter knives and spoons and forks. It all came to better than two dollars, but that was all right. He had the money out of his pay and couldn't think of a better thing to do with it. Then he carried the basket with the stuff in it back to the cafe, and they had his order all fixed and ready for him by the time he got there. Everything fit into the basket just the way he'd planned for it to, and he covered it all with the cloth and carried it outside and down to the creek.

This was kind of exciting, he decided. Him, Billy Ray Halstad, just a working stiff, of course, but sashaying down by the creek-side with a picnic basket on his arm and with a really nice girl down there to see and talk to and nothing bad about it neither.

This was exactly the kind of thing he'd imagined himself doing when he went and daydreamed about having made his mark in the world and being able to live like the swells did. Shee-oot.

He whistled some as he walked and swung the basket in time to a jaunty stride.

Yeah. This was just all-dang-right.

115

Chapter 16

Billy Ray was content. He was lying back with the big piece of cloth spread out under him to keep his shirt from getting dirty. He had his eyes closed and his ankles crossed, and the sunshine felt warm and comfortable. The creek was talking to him softly from a few feet away, and his belly was full.

All the leftover stuff from the picnic except for the cloth he was using to lie back on was already packed away in the basket, and things couldn't have been a whole lot nicer.

That Miss Hattie sure was a nice girl. Polite too. They'd talked quite a while before she excused herself and left. Said she was tired. Billy Ray smiled a little. Likely the poor girl was thirsty too. He had gone and forgotten to get anything for them to drink, but she hadn't said a word of complaint about that.

They had sat right here and talked for

the better part of a couple hours, and Billy Ray had enjoyed it. He'd told her near everything there was to tell about himself, and she had talked some about herself. Not really all that much but some. She was shy. And no wonder, him being a working stiff out of the mines and her being a proper young lady. But she'd sat right there and talked with him and seemed to enjoy the pork chops and biscuits and such he had brought and had never once fussed about not having anything to wash it down with. Billy Ray sighed and turned his face into the sunshine a little better.

Sure would be nice if he could squire her to Sunday services sometime. Walk right in there with Miss Hattie on his arm. Sure would be nice if he could do that.

He was sure. Well, almost sure. That she would go with him if there were services to go to in Blue Gorge. He'd talked to her some more about being saved, and she didn't frown and get fussed up the way the boys in the bunkhouse did.

She'd actually sat right there and *listened* to him, wide-eyed and interested.

She didn't know much about religious stuff, she'd admitted, and that encouraged him to go on an' tell her all the more.

It was a neat feeling, being able to tell

Miss Hattie about it and have her so interested. It made him feel good to be sharing
it, and so quite a bit of their conversation
had been about that.

Shee-oot. What had old Tommy said this
morning? Something about Billy Ray going
and holding his own services up there at
the bunkhouse 'cause there weren't any
regular ones.

And now here he'd gone and done pretty
much the same thing with Miss Hattie.
Why . . .

Billy Ray's eyes snapped open, and he
shot up to a sitting position there on the
stony creek bank.

Something Brother Greer'd said a couple
weeks ago, something about being a wit-
ness to the world . . . He couldn't quite remember what all that little preacher-man
had said, but it'd been something along
those lines.

Billy Ray blinked. He was beginning to
feel trembly, kind of. Excited.

There wasn't any preacher in Blue
Gorge. Not a regular one. That man had
said it might be months before a real
preacher came around again.

And if a fella was going to count himself
saved, why, he oughta be willing to shout
about it, shouldn't he?

He . . . eck, yes, he should.

He'd read something about that just the other night. Couldn't remember exactly what or where, but he was sure he'd read something like that. Someplace in the New Testament, he thought. If that was so it shouldn't be so hard to find again. That was where most of the pages were missing from.

Shee-oot.

Fella could do worse than to stand up and shout for the Lord.

But not just for his own self, now dang it. Not just to make himself look good. A fella could get himself baked to a high crisp if he was pretending to do something for the Lord and was really doing it to set himself up as special, Billy Ray suspected. He didn't want to do that.

Best to get some advice about this before he went and did anything he wasn't supposed to.

If Brother Greer had been handy Billy Ray would have taken the question to him, but there was no telling where Brother Greer had got to in two weeks' time. So that was out. He'd just have to carry this one right straight to the Boss.

Billy Ray wouldn't have admitted it to anybody, but that was the way he'd begun to think about the Lord. It just didn't *feel* right to think of the Lord who'd saved him as some distant power. Not after that talk they'd had on the creek bank when Billy Ray was fretting about the baptism. So he'd kind of got to thinking about the Lord as a boss. Not just some foreman either, but a supervisor.

Another thing he'd have felt uncomfortable about was admitting to how he thought about this Trinity business. Brother Greer had tried to explain that to him, and that part Billy Ray remembered clear enough — about the Father and the Son and the Holy Spirit — so about that one it wasn't that Billy Ray couldn't remember as that he just couldn't get a handle on the thing. Couldn't shake it down out of the Bible either no matter how hard he looked. So he'd solved that one by ignoring it, more or less. Billy Ray solved the problem by thinking about all of Them . . . all of Him? . . . under the one collective term Boss or Lord. That was something he was comfortable with, and as far as he could figure out it didn't seem to make much difference to the Boss, who surely understood that Billy Ray wasn't being any kind of disrespectful when he did it. Besides, a stiff like Billy Ray didn't have to understand it. The Lord did, and that was good enough.

Billy Ray was sitting there on the creek bank where he'd had the picnic with Miss Hattie. Now he swung around until he was on his knees with the fast-running creek in front of him and the mountain peaks all around. He'd scooted off the cloth so that his trousers were getting dirty, but he didn't notice that. He squinched his eyes tight shut and clasped his hands together the way he remembered being taught to do a whole lot of time ago. Praying wasn't something he'd had a bunch of practice at, not even lately when he'd been so busy finding time to read and to talk about being saved, but he was willing to give it a go.

He kind of had the idea that a fellow was supposed to duck his head when he prayed, but he found himself looking up toward the sky although still with his eyes shut. And what he said he said right out loud.

"It's me, Boss. You know. The one you saved a while back. I been thinking, Lord. You know I've always had this feeling that I was supposed to do something special. Well, now I've got to thinking that maybe

You're it. Doing stuff for You, I mean."

This praying business was a little awkward at first, but Billy Ray was beginning to get warmed up to it now. It wasn't really so bad once he got started.

"You know what's going on here. All kinds of wickedness that I wouldn't want to talk about but that I reckon You know about anyhow." Billy Ray paused and took a deep breath. That part had been kind of ticklish. He felt better now that he was through it.

"So what I got to thinking was that maybe You want me to do some telling around here. Just until Brother Greer gets back, that is, I know I ain't so much, being brand new to this salvation business, but if You can do what You done for me, why, I just got to pass that along to other folks. Lord knows . . . oops, excuse me, Lord . . . I mean You already know that there's an awful lot needs to be done around here. And I was thinking, well, maybe I could help out a little. If You want me to, that is. But if You don't, why, let me know somehow so that I won't be going and messing things up. You know?" That was a silly question, Billy Ray realized after he'd said it. Of course He knew. Shee-oot.

"So what I got to say here, I guess, is that

You should just kinda move me around an' use me however You want. I don't mean to set me up as something extra nor make me rich. I just mean that if You want to use me, well. You just up an' have it. I'm willin'." He closed his mouth and thought about it some, nervously aware that the Boss would be listening in on what he was thinking and not just hearing what he was saying, and came to the conclusion that there was probably some more stuff that he ought to throw in there except that he didn't know what all that would be or how to go about it. And as far as what he'd wanted to say went, well, he'd pretty well covered that territory. The Boss was perfectly capable of throwing him down and hollering whoa if Billy Ray was overstepping himself with this idea.

"I guess that's it then, Boss. However You want to roll it, I'll play along."

Billy Ray opened his eyes and stood up, feeling kind of fluttery and scared inside but kind of good too, and brushed off the bits of gravel and sand that were clinging to the fronts of his pant legs.

He finished gathering up the leavings of the picnic things and although he felt a trifle guilty from thinking about it he couldn't help but hope that Miss Hattie would approve of this idea.

Chapter 17

"You? *You* are gonna hold you a preachin' service? Shee-it!" Tommy — and all the rest of the boys too for that matter — were getting an awful kick out of the idea of Billy Ray Halstad holding himself a church service.

"Now I'm sure of it," Tommy said. "You've lost your damned mind, Billy Ray."

Billy Ray smiled at him. "That's the whole point exactly," he said calmly. "I *ain't* damned. Not anymore I ain't. An' you don't hafta be either. Explaining that right there is the whole point o' this." He went back to what he was doing, which was fixing up some signs to post around town.

He had bought some sheets of stiff paper and some pencils and ink, the pencils to outline the writing with and the ink to color in between the lines nice and bold so that the words could be read from a distance, and was busy making up his signs that would bring folks to the service he figured to hold next Sunday morning.

"You're out of your damned mind, Billy Ray," Tommy insisted. Behind him some of the other boys were snorting and snickering and egging him on.

"You boys think what you like," Billy Ray said mildly. There'd been a time when this kind of ragging would have been put a stop to by way of fists and ruffled feathers. It almost surprised even him that he wasn't feeling that way about it now, but it wasn't bothering him a lick. He just went on with what he was doing, and the heck with what anybody else wanted to think about it.

He had quite enough to do, after all, just working out what to write on his signs.

That wasn't near as easy as a body might imagine.

Why, what to call it was itself a problem.

He couldn't actually claim that it was a *church* service, since there wouldn't actually be a preacher there but just another stiff down from the mines with something to say that had to be said. So he couldn't hardly call it an actual church service.

He'd settled on just announcing that there would be a service. Sunday morning. Ten o'clock.

Then there was the problem of where to hold it.

Everybody knew that proper services should be held in a church building or some kind of building or in a big tent or at the very least in a brush arbor.

Billy Ray didn't have any of those available. He couldn't afford to buy a great big tent even if there was one to be found in Blue Gorge, which was doubtful. There sure wasn't any church here nor any building he could borrow or rent that he could think of. About the only places in town big enough to hold a crowd of people would be one of the saloons, and he didn't think it real likely that one of them would be willing to shut down on a day when the stiffs weren't working just so Billy Ray Halstad could hold a service.

Brush arbors were cheap to build, of course. They just took some work to make. And while Billy Ray was more than willing enough to put in some work on this project there was also the consideration that there wasn't any brush to speak of left within a couple miles of Blue Gorge. Any hunks of brush big enough to make an arbor from had long since been chopped down and burnt for firewood. Finding wood to burn or to build with was always a problem anywhere around a mining camp because wood was scarce and everything available would be pretty well used up and gone within a few months after a camp got started. So the idea of a brush arbor was pretty much out of the question too.

Billy Ray had decided that about the only thing left for him to do would be to just go down to where Brother Greer had set his tent up that time and hold his services in the open air. Anybody that wanted to sit could bring something to sit on.

So he settled for lettering on his signs: Services. Sunday. 10 a.m. On the open ground below town.

He thought about it some more and added: All welcome.

That should do it, he decided. He finished the lettering on his first sign, got the outlines drawn and held it up so he could look it over. Satisfied, he got to work on the next one. Now all he had to do was copy that first sign a couple dozen times and get them all inked and then go down of an evening to tack them up around town.

He was feeling pretty eager about it all. This was the biggest and the best thing Billy Ray had ever got himself involved in.

Rick Price, who was a mucker on the

Four Level crew, sidled over and looked at the sign over Billy Ray's shoulder. He gave the other boys a wink and poked Billy Ray in the shoulder.

"What're you up to, Halstad? Gonna take up a collection Sunday? I seen you in action, you know, bub. If you get any money out o' the good folks, you'll just turn around and spend it on some hoor over at Miss Charlotte's. Is that what you got in mind, Halstad?"

Billy Ray ignored the needling. It didn't bother him a lick. Which in itself was some kind of record. He'd whipped Rick Price's butt before over less than this, but now he didn't even want to.

Billy Ray just went on with what he was doing and pretended that the rest of the boys weren't even in the place.

Chapter 18

Billy Ray was almighty tired. He'd stayed up half of last night finishing the last of his posters and then spent part of the rest of it trying to make some sense of the so often strange words printed on the flimsy pages of his Bible. It had occurred to him, kind of late in the game but at least before the last second arrived, that come Sunday he would be expected to have something to say, so he was trying to get some reading in before then. He'd kept at it until the words started swimming off the sides of the pages and he'd figured it was about time to get some sleep.

Now, his shift over and his bunk calling out to him like a long-lost love, he was down in town again.

What with being tired and dirty and sore and another shift coming around practically before a fellow had time to blink, even the youngest and randiest of the boys seldom had the energy to get down to Blue

Gorge during the week. Weekday trade in the town was mostly left to fellas in easy jobs or to a few hardy stiffs from the closest in of the mines. But this was too important to let go, so Billy Ray had made the walk down the twisty path and was stifling yawns while he worked.

He'd bought a tack hammer — forty-five cents at Brightman's — and had half a mouthful of carpet tacks that he was using to pin his posters up. He laid his sheaf of posters on the ground and set a rock on top of them to secure them from the evening breeze, then commenced to pound one of them up on the sidewall of "Doc" Hoosier's pharmacy. So far as Billy Ray knew nobody in town actually believed that the man's name was Hoosier, but most were willing to accept that he probably came from Indiana, whatever his name might have been back there. Doc was patronized by everybody, stiffs and swells alike, for two reasons. One was that he had never actually poisoned anybody with the medications he made up to his own notions of need — there not being a real doctor in Blue Gorge — and the other because Doc's was the only pharmacy in the gorge and therefore the only place where a fellow could buy anything for miseries that didn't come out of a catalog.

Billy Ray nailed up the top corners of his poster and was working on securing the bottom when Doc came charging outside with his face red and a stout pestle in his fist like he was as ready to grind a head as a medication.

"What the hell are you . . . oh." Doc came to a stop in front of Billy Ray's sign and tipped his head back a bit so he could see it clear through the spectacles that hung off the end of his nose. "Oh."

"You don't mind, do you, Mr. Hoosier?"

"No, I don't mind. Not for that. But you could've asked before you started hammering on my wall." Doc looked kind of sheepishly down toward the pestle he was carrying for a weapon and shoved the thing into his back pocket.

"I thought you were closed for the evening," Billy Ray said. "Next time I'll ask first."

"No, you go right ahead. I just thought you were up to some silliness. You can put this kind of notice up anytime you like." Doc turned his head toward Billy Ray and tipped it back again so that he could get a better look at him. "I've seen you before, haven't I?"

"You've seen everybody in Blue Gorge

131

before. That's why I wanted to put a sign here. Everybody comes to you some time or another, Mr. Hoosier."

Hoosier accepted that as a compliment of sorts and smiled a little. "Go on with what you're doing, young man. But I suggest you ask before you pound elsewhere. It wouldn't do to get yourself bashed by mistake."

"Yes, sir. Thank you for the advice, sir."

Hoosier went back inside his shop, and Billy Ray finished with his chore. The pharmacist's advice was probably good, but having to spend that kind of time finding people and getting permissions would sure make the job a longer one. And he was tired enough without that too.

Still, it was nice to realize that he wasn't getting the kind of razzing from the towns-people that he was coming to expect from the stiffs back in the bunkhouse. Doc had sure been pleasant about it anyhow. Billy Ray picked up his stack of posters and went on down the street. A sign in every block was what was needed, he figured, and more up at the honky-tonk end of town where the boys came down to play. Billy Ray couldn't think of anybody who needed to get the word more than the stiffs and the sporting women who also lived up at that end of town.

Come to think of it . . .

It was kinda like that old recipe for rabbit stew. First you catch the rabbit. Same thing here, Billy Ray figured. If you wanta tame some lions, first you gotta go into the den and get their attention.

That way of putting it pleased him because he kinda remembered hearing once a story about some fella from the Old Testament times going into a lion's den. He couldn't remember that whole story now, but he was sure there was something to that effect someplace in the Old Testament. One of these times, when he wasn't so sleepy, he was going to have to see if he couldn't just look that one up and get refreshed on what it was all about.

Meantime he marched straight up the street to Miss Charlotte's place and put up *two* posters there.

And a bunch more in that neighborhood.

He even went over to Crib Row and pounded some up over there. It wasn't a particularly busy evening there, and pretty soon he had the attention of all the working girls of that neighborhood. None of them came out and talked to him about what he was doing, but he couldn't help but notice that he never had time to get more than a few paces away from a nailed-up poster before some of the girls came slipping out to take a look at what he was doing. The ones of them that could read passed the word around to those that couldn't, and while not a one of them ever actually came and spoke to him there seemed to be a lot of chattering going on behind his back.

Billy Ray felt pretty well pleased with himself by the time the last of his posters was put up and he was able to climb back up toward the Chagra No. 1 and a little sleep before his next shift started.

Chapter 19

Billy Ray was praying. He probably should have been praying for strength, guidance, wisdom. Stuff like that. What he was praying for was rain. What he wanted was a real gully washer of a thunderstorm. Or a sudden blizzard. A blizzard would do. Or a tornado. Any dang thing to get him out of this thing that he'd gone and started.

He hadn't eaten anything since supper last night, and now he was wishing he hadn't had that. He was so scared and so nervous that he was sure he was going to stand right there in front of everybody and throw up.

He paced back and forth and wrung his hands together. That didn't make him feel any better but at least it gave him something to do while he was feeling so miserable.

It was nearly time, and he could see some people drifting down the street toward the open patch of ground where he was fixing to make a fool of himself.

Every single one of them that he could see was dressed better than he was. He didn't own a suit or nice coat and so was standing there in his shirt sleeves, but every one of the men he could see were wearing suits. He should at least have had his good shirt washed and starched again, but it was too late to be thinking about that.

He shuddered. Thinking about his dang shirt was better than thinking about what was about to happen here. Whoo-boy. He felt his belly knot and his gorge begin to rise, and he swallowed several times, hard and fast and deliberate, trying to force it all back. His knees felt weak and trembly, and he was sure he must be dripping sweat so bad that anybody could see. He could feel it running down his sides from under his arms, and it a cool morning.

Jesus!

He wasn't being disrespectful. He was praying again but so scared he couldn't get his thoughts formed into words even for that.

If any of these dang people shouted boo he was going to turn and run.

He turned his back toward the people

that were drifting down toward the meeting place and clamped his hands together and squinched his eyes tight shut.

"Jesus." It was all he could think to say at the time. After a bit there didn't seem much point in putting it off any longer. He couldn't make it go away anyhow. He put his hands down to his sides and tried to stop his shaking and turned around to face them.

Oh Lordy. That wasn't being disrespectful either. All of what he was trying to say and couldn't, he at least meant it sincerely.

He tried to smile toward the folks and felt like his face was fixing to crack and split in half and fall off into the dirt, one half on each side, one half laying beside each soot-blacked shoe.

He kind of wished it would fall off because that would give him an excuse to not say anything. They could just carry him back up to his bunk, and he could forget this business.

He rolled his eyes up and asked, "Lord, are you gonna give me a hand with this?"

The Lord didn't say anything.

Billy Ray looked down.

It was a strange bunch of people that had seen his posters and come down to the meeting place.

Not at all the folks he would have expected to see here.

There weren't any stiffs down from the mines, for instance. Not a one. And no women that looked like any of the sporting girls off the line, and if the truth be told Billy Ray would have recognized most if not quite all of that sort. There wasn't a single one of them neither.

What he had out there was a little group of eight or ten women — he blinked a couple times and counted them, giving him something solid to concentrate on for the moment, and found that he'd been close; there were seven women — who were wives or whatever but definitely from the better element of Blue Gorge.

They hadn't brought anything to sit on and were all standing together in a tight clutch like so many hens, all of them glancing about now and then to give some suspicious glances toward the men who had come and were standing apart in several other tight little bunches.

Over to the right there was a group of men who'd come without their wives and who were dressed extra fancy for Blue Gorge, suits and vests and gold watch chains. These men all looked prosperous and had to have their vests tailored full to go over their bellies. They looked several cuts above mere supervisors, managers, or more, and were not a crowd that Billy Ray would have expected to see at services, especially without their wives along. Billy Ray had seen most of them before but always from a distance and certainly never to speak to.

Then standing well apart from them there were two other, smaller groups of men. Three in one clutch and two in another.

The bunch of three looked like maybe working stiffs dressed above themselves. Like they weren't comfortable in tight collars and ties. Billy Ray recognized one of them. It was the little man who'd approached him in the cafe that time and asked him about the Wobblies, whoever the heck they were. Now here the fellow was coming to services and bringing two friends with him.

And standing about as far away from that bunch as they could get and still be considered to be a part of the crowd were a pair of stiffs who'd slid in when Billy Ray wasn't looking. Seeing them there almost made him feel better, because they were dressed no better than he was.

Billy Ray didn't recognize either of them

so they sure didn't come down from the Chagra No. 1. They must've been new to the camp because if he had ever seen either of them before he would have remembered it. They were both great big, burly fellows who looked like they'd have done just fine in a prizefighting ring but would likely bash their heads if they tried to stand upright and walk through a mine shaft. They were that big. They looked bored too, which he thought kinda strange for men going to services.

He was about to have to get started but found an excuse to delay it a bit more to wait on a couple more men who were walking down from town. These fellows were fairly well-dressed too but didn't look so prosperous as the first bunch of men. They were just a little seedier and not quite so clean, and one of them looked like he was still carrying some of last night's load.

That was sure all right, though. Billy Ray'd gone and found salvation when he was in a condition like that himself, so he sure couldn't claim that the Lord sneered at a sinner.

If that was so, why, there wouldn't be any point to any of this.

Which, by dang, was what he should go and tell these folks.

That thought came to him with considerable relief. He'd had a whole week to work out what he was going to say here this morning, and he hadn't got any kind of a handle on it. Nothing. But that fellow coming down to hear and kind of swaying and staggering while he walked, that put the idea into Billy Ray's head that all he would have to do would be to tell these folks what had happened to him just a few weeks ago, right here on this same spot, and then see what happened next.

He felt better. Not good, certainly, but better.

He took a deep breath, squeezed his eyes shut for a moment of silent, wordless pleading — he couldn't pretend that it was prayer; he was outright begging and both he and the Lord knew it — and began to talk.

"Folks," he said in a voice loud enough to cover the quavering in his tone, "I'm no preacher-man like was here a while back. But I got something to tell you. Something really fine. Which is why I called you down here on a Sunday morning."

Even while he was talking, the words kind of coming out of his mouth now without him hardly thinking about it, it was occurring to him that there was no sign this morning of Miss Hattie Markle. He was disappointed by that and hoped she would still be down by the creek when he got done here.

Then there wasn't any time for him to be thinking about such. He set in to telling these people about what had happened to him when Brother Greer had his tent on this spot and what a fine, fine thing that could be for anybody that was willing to accept the personal salvation the Good Lord was willing to give away free of charge.

Chapter 20

"That was inspiring, Brother Halstad. Positively inspiring." The lady took his hand in both of hers and squeezed.

Billy Ray was so startled that he almost swallowed his own tongue. He did choke and cough some.

Brother Halstad? Nobody had ever called him anything like that before. Nobody'd called him anything remotely like that and he certainly hadn't thought of himself as Brother anybody. Shee-oot, that was something you called a preacher.

"Lordy," he mumbled, and this time he had to admit that it wasn't any kind of praying. He was just so startled he blurted it right out.

The lady — the other women who'd come with her were pressed all around him in a sort of circle and they were reaching for his hands and patting his shoulders too while the first one talked — never seemed to notice Billy Ray's disrespectful lapse.

"I hope you will give your testimony again next week, Brother Halstad," she was saying.

Which startled Billy Ray just about as bad as her calling him Brother had done. He hadn't given any thought to there being a next week. It had dang near killed him from losing sleep over this week. Now these ladies were acting like they expected this to be a regular thing.

"My husband will be here next week, Brother Halstad," the lady was saying. "And I do so want him to hear your testimony." She lowered her voice a bit. "He drinks, you see. Now and then. I want him to hear how a gentleman can be saved from the demon rum as you were, Brother Halstad."

"My husband should hear it too, Brother Halstad," another of the women said over the first one's shoulder.

"You can count on seeing more gentlemen here next week," a third piped into it.

"My husband shall certainly be here," one of them said firmly. She said it low and serious, and Billy Ray knew dang good and well that that fellow would be here or dang well suffer some consequences. He wouldn't want to be in that man's shoes if the poor soul tried to refuse. Huh uh.

"Do you think we could sing some hymns next week, Brother Halstad?" one of the women asked.

"Well, ma'am, I, uh." Billy Ray felt his cheeks heating up. "I don't exactly know any hymns, ma'am. Don't know any songs at all that could be sung in decent company."

"You certainly know plenty, Melba," another woman said. "And you could get Harry to bring his squeeze-box to accompany you."

Another lady took up the idea and carried it further. "We could get together this week and practice some hymns, Melba. We could start a regular choir. If Brother Halstad approves, of course."

The whole dang bunch of them turned to stare at Billy Ray.

"Why, yes ma'am, ladies, I think that would be a fine idea. Miss Melba could lead the singing?"

None of them seemed to notice Billy Ray's uncertainties. They jumped on the idea and wallowed in it.

They all spent some more time telling him how inspired they'd been, but that was just for form. Their hearts weren't in it any longer. They were too busy now planning the choir they were fixing to bring to Brother Halstad's services.

"Oh Lord," Billy Ray muttered as the ladies excused themselves and chirped and chattered their way up the street.

This time he did say it with the proper intent.

Next Sunday.

"Oh Lord."

He blinked a few times and looked around.

All of the ladies had come up to speak with him after, but every one of the men had gone and disappeared while he was talking with the women. Billy Ray had to wonder if he'd done any good talking to them. After all, it was pretty obvious that the ladies were already saved. It was those who weren't that he'd really wanted to get through to.

Still and all, it looked like he would have another shot at them next Sunday. If they chose to come back, that is. He hoped they would.

He stood there for a minute, just thinking, then glanced up toward the sun to check the time as he didn't own a watch.

It was getting on toward noon, and Miss

Hattie might not still be down along the creek. He hurried that way, but he was too late. He couldn't tell from just looking if she might've been there or not. If she was, she didn't leave him a note or any sign that she'd been expecting him.

Disappointed in one way but kind of excited in another — after all, his first service had gone kinda well — he turned and started the long hike back up to the bunkhouse.

This Sunday afternoon he figured to *sleep*, by golly. And woe unto the poor stiff that tried to keep him from it.

Brother Billy Ray Halstad smiled some as he walked back up to the Chagra No. 1. It had just occurred to him that that lady had actually referred to Billy Ray Halstad as a gentleman. That was another first, right up there alongside of being called Brother.

And they'd gone and asked him was it all right for them to start a choir. Shee-oot.

This was more fun than he'd ever expected it could be. Why, he was even looking forward to next Sunday's service now.

Chapter 21

Man, this preaching business was more work than Billy Ray ever would have expected. After a full day's shift on the hoist a fella wanted to get in some sleep and some relaxation, but it seemed that there was always lots to do.

He had to keep an eye on those dang signs, for instance. The dang things were always needing to be replaced, either because the old ones fell down or blew down or plain and simple were torn down.

And like on Thursday night he went down with some fresh signs he'd made up, and Mrs. Horvath, who he remembered from Sunday but whose name he hadn't known then, collared him outside the haberdashery where he'd just bought another good shirt and a secondhand coat that would more or less go with his good trousers.

"Brother Halstad," she piped up, sounding real pleased to see him. "Sister Elizabeth has been ailing, Brother Halstad. I know it would be a great comfort to her if you could come visit with her and pray with her."

"Yes, ma'am." This wasn't anything Billy Ray had thought of doing, but it was clearly the sort of thing he ought to do if he was going to be holding services and whatever.

So he went along with Mrs. Horvath and was taken right inside the Kuntz home down at the decent end of town, the first time Billy Ray — or for that matter anybody he knew of from up at the mines — had ever been invited inside such a place.

Mrs. Kuntz's husband, who Billy Ray thought was a geologist from the Margaret Mae way up toward the head of the gorge, actually jumped up and looked flustered about Billy Ray Halstad coming to call and dang near knocked over the toddy that he thought he was hiding from "Brother" Halstad. Billy Ray got kind of a kick out of that but managed to not crack a smile, looking all solemn and serious when he was led back to the bedroom where Sister Elizabeth was tucked in under a heavy coverlet with a bunch of pillows plumped up at her back and a tray nearby with smelling salts and some of Doc Hoosier's medications and on top of the covers beside her a great big Bible bound all in leather and with gilt lettering on the cover that was too small for Billy Ray to see from the distance.

She looked just as glad to see him as Mrs. Horvath had been and clung onto his hand and cried some and said how glad she was that he'd come to pray with her.

Well, after that there wasn't anything Billy Ray could do but to sit and pray with her. Which he did.

Mrs. Kuntz claimed that she felt considerable better afterward, and that pleased everybody, including Billy Ray, who really didn't know quite what he was doing there but was willing if that was what the Lord wanted him to do.

"I hope you'll be feeling up to singing next Sunday," Billy Ray told her.

"I certainly plan on it, Brother Halstad. All of us have been working on our songs, Sister Melba in particular. But we are all taking our duties quite seriously. You'll see come Sunday."

"Did you want to approve our list of selections beforehand?" Mrs. Horvath asked.

"Oh, uh, no'm. I don't reckon that would be necessary."

Both ladies positively beamed at the confidence Billy Ray was placing in them all.

It was all Billy Ray could do to keep from shaking his head in wonder when he left the room.

And then once he was back out to the parlor Mr. Kuntz, who was a real gentleman and not just some stiff down from the mines, he got flustered again and sputtered something about offering, uh, Brother Halstad something to eat or maybe some dessert and coffee.

Billy Ray knew better than to press his luck. He'd just go and spoil everything by doing something dumb if he hung around here, like spilling the coffee in his lap or dropping crumbs on the rug or something. So he smiled real polite and acted like this sort of thing happened just all the time and then got out of there *fast* before any of that could happen.

By the time he got back outside to where he could settle down and think again he was about half convinced that he was getting away with something here, though he didn't quite know what.

What he felt like, he guessed, was some kind of imposter, pretending to be something he wasn't. And getting away with it. That was the thing. Getting away with it.

This time, in private, he did shake his head some as he walked back up toward town.

If he tried to tell any of the boys back at the bunkhouse about all this they'd hoot him down and call him a liar. What's more, he wouldn't blame them if they did. Coffee and dessert, indeed. Shee-oot.

Chapter 22

"Brother Halstad. Wait a minute."

"Yes?" Billy Ray stopped and rearranged his packages from his right arm to his left so he would have a hand free. It had come dark while he was in the Kuntz home and so it took him a moment to recognize the man who was approaching. It was the little fellow who'd spoken to him in the cafe that time and then showed up for services last Sunday. "Of course, you're Mister, uh . . ."

The little man, who still looked seedy but not quite so much so as the first time Billy Ray had seen him, stepped up to him and shook. "Murphy," he said. "Lemuel K. Murphy."

"Um. Yes. I was pleased to see you Sunday, Mr. Murphy. More workin' boys ought to hear the good Lord's word, you know. So I was real pleased to see you an' your friends there Sunday." Billy Ray started walking again, slower this time with

Lemuel K. Murphy walking alongside him. He almost missed the look that Murphy gave him. It was kind of amazed and kind of amused, both at the same time, which didn't make any sense. But then Billy Ray was getting awfully close to deciding that nothing made much sense anyhow, so he didn't worry about it.

"Yes, well, uh, it was a pleasure for us too," Murphy said, sounding like he didn't particularly mean it.

That was all right. Billy Ray darn sure would have been skeptical about this salvation stuff too if he hadn't experienced it for himself. Skeptical? Shoot, he'd have given the horselaugh to anybody that suggested such a thing to him before he stumbled onto Brother Greer that day. So Murphy was being more polite about it than Billy Ray would've been himself not so very long ago. He guessed he could understand that and get along with it all right. "Was there something you wanted, Mr. Murphy? I don't know all that much, but I'm sure here an' ready to share whatever I do know about the Lord."

"In a manner of speaking, Brother Halstad. In a manner of speaking. Would you have a few minutes?"

"Sure." Billy Ray was already so tired

that a little more time wasn't going to hurt anything.

"In here then," Murphy said. He took Billy Ray by the elbow and guided him toward the poorer of Blue Gorge's two hotels. It was the sort of place where strays would put up on the cheap until they either found work or drifted downmountain.

The place was as much saloon as it was hotel, and Billy Ray felt a little uncomfortable going inside it. He hadn't set foot into such a place since the day he was saved, and he was a bit awkward about it now.

"My room is just upstairs," Murphy assured him, pulling him on through the door and past the crowd of drinkers in the space that would have been a lobby in most hotels.

The room was no great shakes, but at least in there Billy Ray couldn't smell the beer or hear the customers talking. The beer had smelled better than he thought it would, and it kind of got him to wanting just one short one to soothe his throat and take some of the tired off him.

Murphy seated him on a wooden chair in the room and looked around like he'd forgotten where he left something. "I don't have anything to offer you that a reverend would want," he said.

"That's all right. Besides, I'm not a real reverend. Just another stiff that's seen the light."

Murphy grunted and turned away to root down in the bottom of a Gladstone bag that was sitting at the foot of the bed.

"How much do you know about Jesus, Mr. Murphy?" Billy Ray asked, assuming that that was what the man wanted to talk about. He had, after all, been to services so he must have questions, must be looking for what Billy Ray'd found.

"Nothing," Murphy said impatiently. "That is . . . that isn't what I wanted to talk to you about. Right now." He gave up looking inside the bag and went to a drawer in a bureau in the corner. "Ah. Here 'tis." He pulled out some papers, selected a pamphlet from among them, and shoved it toward Billy Ray.

"What's this?"

"It's something you ought to read, Brother Halstad. Any reverend that cares a thing about his, uh, flock ought to be up on this subject. If you intend to do your Christian duty, Reverend Halstad, it is your God-given duty to support our work and make conditions humane for the working man."

"But what is it?" Billy Ray really didn't

156

want to get trapped into promising to read whatever this odd little man was pushing. It was bad enough trying to wade through the Bible one word at a time. Which was something he probably should start praying about. He sure did need to get better at this reading business. It was hard, slow work at the best of times for him. Taking on any extra was something he'd rather not have to do.

"It's about decency, Reverend Halstad," Murphy said.

"I'm not a . . ."

Murphy wasn't listening. He was doing some preaching of his own, or so he sounded. "It is about human liberty, Reverend Halstad. And a man's right to make a decent wage for himself and not have to suffer the threat of death or maiming while he's doing so. It's about the struggle of the working class to survive the oppression of capitalistic managers who care only about profits and stockholder dividends but who care nothing about the working man. It is about . . ."

This time it was Billy Ray who wasn't listening. He stood and handed Murphy back his pamphlet. "I'm sorry, Mr. Murphy, but I'm just an ol' boy down from the mines who's found the way. I don't know anything 'bout this."

"Exactly!" Murphy cried, his eyes aflame with a passion very much like that Billy Ray had seen in Brother Greer's when the preacher-man talked about the Lord. "Exactly, Reverend Halstad," Murphy said. "You don't know. You need to know. This is your Christian duty, Reverend Halstad. Your Christian duty."

"I don't know all that much, Mr. Murphy, but I ain't so dumb as to mistake the fact that my Christian duty is to Christ the Lord an' not to some cause that I don't understand."

"But you must understand . . ."

"No, sir," Billy Ray said slowly. "I know what you're getting at now. You're one o' them union fellows. Well, I don't know much about unions. They sound like an awful fine idea. But everything I've heard about them is trouble, Mr. Murphy. Boys that wanta work getting thrown outta their jobs, either by the bosses getting mad and shutting down or by the unions getting mad and shutting things down or by the government getting mad at both sides and shutting things down. No, sir. I reckon until somebody comes up with a better way than what's been tried so far, I don't reckon it would be my Christian duty to be telling people that you're right or that you're wrong either one. So I'll leave you your paper, Mr. Murphy, an' be on my way."

"But you are so wrong, Reverend Halstad . . ."

"I been trying to tell you, Mr. Murphy, that I ain't no reverend. I'm just me. A guy that's got himself saved, thanks to grace an not works, and no power to me because of it. Let me tell you about that, Mr. Murphy. Let me tell you what the Lord can do for you . . ."

Murphy took the pamphlet from Billy Ray's hand, folded it over, and shoved it into Billy Ray's pocket. "We'll talk again sometime, Brother Halstad. Just take the literature. Read it when you have a chance. Show it to your friends and see what they think of it. Don't give me an answer now. We'll talk about it again later."

"What I think we should ought to talk about later is your salvation, Mr. Murphy."

"That too, reverend. We'll talk about that too." Murphy seemed anxious now to get him out of the hotel room, perhaps before Billy Ray could change his mind and insist on returning the paper or insist on telling the odd little man about the Lord or for whatever reason. Now Murphy was practically pushing Billy Ray out of his room. "We will talk about it again another time, reverend."

Billy Ray sighed and decided not to bother trying to correct Murphy again. The man just didn't want to listen.

"I, uh, maybe I'll see you Sunday, Mr. Murphy."

"Of course, reverend. Sure thing."

Billy Ray tucked his packages under his arm and hurried downstairs and out through the saloon, the sounds and the smells of the place presenting reminders that he really did not want.

Lordy, but he was tired now. The walk back up to the Chagra No. 1 seemed impossibly long from down at this end of the path. But standing there fretting about it was not going to get the path climbed. But then all he had to do, really, was take one step. At a time.

He headed slowly toward home.

Chapter 23

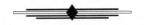

She was there, thank goodness. He had been afraid he would be too early coming before the service or, like last week, too late if he waited until after. But she was there already.

Billy Ray stopped at the top of the bank — instead of coming the usual way down the creek he had taken the quicker route down the road and then cut across toward the stream — and stood there for a minute just looking at her.

Miss Hattie hadn't heard him, he didn't think. Probably couldn't over the sound of the water pouring over the rocks. She was sitting with her back to him, her knees drawn up toward her chin and her arms wrapped around them. She was looking off toward the peaks, toward where the slanting morning light was bright and bold on some white streaks of leftover snowbanks. It was an awfully pretty sight.

But then the one he was interested in was even prettier.

It amazed him now that he had ever thought Miss Hattie plain.

Looking at her now he couldn't even remember why he might have thought it.

She wasn't plain. Just delicate. And really very pretty.

He couldn't see her face from this angle, of course, but then he didn't need to. He could remember every curve and every texture and every hint of color in her eyes and cheeks and throat. And in her lips. He shouldn't be thinking about that, he knew, but he did. A lot. Times when he'd be done with his reading for the night and the other boys long since abed and snoring and him so tired his eyes felt like they'd been sanded, why, he would lay awake for the longest time yet, seeing Miss Hattie's face in his mind's eye.

And if the truth be told thinking about what it would be like to kiss her.

Billy Ray blushed. Standing there at the top of the creek bank and looking down at her unaware of him being behind her and thinking about those night-thoughts, he felt embarrassed for the things he'd been thinking and began to blush in spite of himself.

He really would like to kiss her, though. And admitting that to himself he blushed all the harder.

That was a worrisome thought in a way. Brother Billy Ray Halstad, who certainly should have had better control of himself now that he was saved and standing up in front of strangers to speak out for the Lord . . . Brother Billy Ray Halstad had never in his life even once kissed a girl.

He had done other things with girls. Just about everything he'd ever heard of that a fella *could* do with a girl he'd sampled at least once. Most things many more times than once.

But none of that had been with a decent girl. Not hardly. And there were some kinds of girls that a fellow just didn't kiss.

So in all his life Billy Ray had never really kissed a girl, not counting Lucy what's-her-name whose family had lived about a half mile away when Billy Ray was growing up. He didn't count that time because he had only been nine or ten and Lucy a bit younger than that, and they'd been more playing and experimenting than kissing. Although he had gotten some welts from it that he could still remember when dang Lucy told her mother, who told her father, who told Billy Ray's father. It was kind of funny now, remembering it, but it sure hadn't been funny at the time.

But except for Lucy that long-ago time, he was no experienced hand at kissing, and the thought of it, with a decent girl like Hattie, pulled at him in two very different directions.

Billy Ray got hold of himself and forced such thoughts out of his mind. He was acting downright previous to be thinking such things, and there was just no need for it.

He picked up a small rock and chunked it into the creek in front of where Miss Hattie was looking.

She saw the splash, jumped a little from the surprise of it, and turned around quick. When she saw who it was she smiled.

That smile made Billy Ray feel better than silly thoughts about kissing her had. He ran down the steep-sided bank in a flurry of falling gravel until he came near enough that they could hear one another over the sound of the water.

"I missed you last week," he said.

"I was here."

"So was I but not until late. I, uh, had services last Sunday." He tried to say it like it wasn't anything special, but even he

164

could hear that he was sounding proud about it. That probably was a wrong thing to do, but he couldn't help it.

"You did? Billy Ray, I'm so proud of you."

He grinned at her and pointed a red-eared, aw-shucks look down toward his shoes. "We're gonna have them again this morning. In fact, the way some folks are taking it, I think they're gonna expect services as a regular thing now. We're starting a choir and everything. I, uh, was hoping you could come. And then afterward, well, maybe I could get another picnic lunch and we could come down here to eat it." There. He'd gotten it all out. This morning he'd been more nervous about finding Miss Hattie and asking her that than he was about speaking at services.

"Oh, Billy Ray. I'd love to. But I can't."

"You can't," he repeated.

She looked away from him. "No. I can't."

"Is it because I'm not a real preacher?"

"Don't be silly. I'd love to hear you. I just can't."

"It was all right for you to go to services when Brother Greer was speaking," he pointed out.

"Brother Greer?"

"You know. When I was saved. You were there."

"No, I wasn't."

"But you . . ." He shook his head, totally confused now. "I thought you were," he said lamely.

"No," she said. Then she smiled. "But I could wait here 'til you're done. We could still have that picnic if you want."

"You'd wait all that time?"

She nodded. There was something in her expression, in her eyes, and in the set of her mouth, that was almighty pleasing. Encouraging too, except that a gentleman, particularly a gentleman who'd been saved, didn't take advantage. Not that Billy Ray considered himself to be a gentleman. But he was doing his best to act like one.

"I can't tell you exactly how long it'll be," he said.

"That's all right. I'll wait for you."

"You won't forget."

Miss Hattie laughed. "I won't forget."

"Yeah, well, I better get back. Are you sure you can't come?"

"I'm sorry, Billy Ray. I truly can't."

"All right, then." But he was going to have to do some talking with her, by dang, about getting herself right with the Lord and going to services.

That could wait, though. They would talk about that later. While they were having their picnic.

He hesitated, not wanting to leave quite yet but knowing that he should.

Hattie reached out and touched her fingertips to the back of his hand. Just that little bit of a touch jolted him. "Go on," she said. "I'll be here when you get back."

Billy Ray turned and ran up the creek bank, slipping and sliding a little and getting his freshly polished shoes even dustier than they'd gotten coming down. He stopped at the top to turn and wave to her, then loped off up the road toward where the folks would be gathering, choir and all, to hear the services.

Chapter 24

"Very, uh, nice service, Brother Halstad," Melba Small's husband said. His wife was standing behind him, carrying the concertina he had used to provide the music for the hymn singing.

"Mostly thanks to you and your missus," Billy Ray said modestly. Although he had to admit to himself that he'd been truly pleased with the way things had gone this morning — quite apart from being able to have another picnic with Miss Hattie, that is. There'd been more people today, more ladies showing up and most of them bringing their menfolk along with them. He had even thought that Harry Small was enjoying the opportunity to play and to sing along with the ladies. Now the man was acting just a bit nervous.

Then Billy Ray saw what was likely wrong. "You can go ahead an' fire 'er up, Mr. Small. It wouldn't be respectful to smoke in a church, I agree, but this ain't a church and the Lord already knows you smoke."

"You don't mind?"

"If He don't mind, Mr. Small, I sure don't. I figure if He wants to tell you otherwise, He'll find His own way to do it. He never said anything to me about it anyhow."

Small laughed and began to load his briar in a hurry.

Billy Ray looked past him. Most of the other men, all of the single ones anyway, had already gone.

That was kind of a curious thing, Billy Ray was thinking. How there were so many little groups of single fellows again today, but just like last week they hadn't participated much nor seemed to get much out of what he was saying. They'd just listened, real serious looking and almost sour. And when the choir sang they hadn't so much as tried to join in.

There had been a smaller group of rich-looking men than last week but those same two big stiffs and Murphy with his same friends. Those three little groups had all acted like they were trying to ignore one another and dang near like they were trying to ignore Billy Ray too. Curious.

Not his worry, though. They were sure welcome, and if they got some sort of message out of it in spite of themselves, well, that was the Lord's affair. Billy Ray sure wasn't going to question it.

"Will we see you again next week, Mr. Small?"

Small thought about that for a few seconds. Then he smiled. "Yeah. Yeah, I think you will, Brother Halstad. You aren't so damn narrow-minded like some I've heard. Yeah, I think I will come back."

From a few feet behind him his wife, who hadn't looked like she was listening as she was busy talking with Mrs. Horvath, snorted. "I could have told you that, Brother Halstad."

"Good. You ladies certainly did a fine job this morning. Mighty fine. Why, I'll bet there's not a regular church down in Denver, no matter how big or fancy, that had singing this morning to match what we had here. No, ma'am, not one of them could've."

Melba Small and the other ladies pretended embarrassment but preened with pleasure over that comment. And every one of them heard it. They were trying to look like they weren't listening, but they were.

"My man will be here too, Brother Halstad," Mrs. Kuntz said. "He won't lay abed another Sunday, let me tell you."

"Yes'm, but I reckon you and me shouldn't be too quick to judge. Does the Lord want him here, why, He can shake 'im out and set him to running."

"And if I'm led to be the instrument of that shaking out, Brother Halstad?"

"Then by all means, ma'am, you go where you're led. You shouldn't let anybody, me the least of all as I'm just a sinner my own self, take you anyplace but where you're led to be."

"That's a strange kind of preaching, mister," one of the men put in. Billy Ray couldn't remember whose husband this one was, but he knew he belonged to one of the ladies. "Most I've heard . . . no, dammit . . . all the preachers I've heard before would have every answer to every question. And most of them before the question's even been asked."

"I wouldn't know about that. An' maybe I'm wrong or something. I just know that I been saved, been given the gift of salvation, and I want to tell folks about that. But I'm no preacher-man. I don't claim to be. All I can tell you is what I believe is right, you see. I sure can't make any claims to bein'

better than anybody else, though, or knowing what everybody else in the world
oughta do. Why, I got troubles enough
trying to figure out how I oughta act."

"What do you think about strong drink,
Halstad?"

No "brother" included. The man was
testing him and was perfectly willing to go
on the prod once Billy Ray answered.

"For you or for me?"

"Wouldn't the answer be the same?"

Billy Ray shook his head. "Nope. The
answer for me is pretty simple. I can't
handle the beer. It's that that I was fleein'
from when I got saved. So for me personal
I would have to say that I ought to leave it
be. For you, though, well . . . that you got
to take up with the Boss. I recall that
someplace in Proverbs . . . other places
too . . . it warns against getting drunk. But
if it says anything about drink, why, I ain't
found that yet."

"Jesus's first miracle was turning water
into wine for that wedding party," Mrs.
Kuntz said. She sounded hesitant, though,
like she really did not want to admit it.

"Was it? I'll have to look that one up."
Billy Ray turned back to the man who was
expecting to get a snootful of fire and
brimstone. "See there? I sure ain't about to

claim that He done anything wrong. So I guess that one you got to take up direct."

The man grunted, looking half pleased and the other half maybe a little bit disappointed.

"If you folks would excuse me now . . . ?"

Billy Ray hurried toward the cafe. He was looking forward to this afternoon more than he wanted to admit to himself.

Chapter 25

Billy Ray felt it more than he heard it. More a quick increase in the pressure on his ears than a sound, really. A moment later there was a puff of dust coming up from the shaft opening and spreading through the place as the sudden pressure, racing like an artificial wind through the tunnels and up the shaft, drove the rock dust along with it. Somewhere down below one of the crews had fired a charge, knocking down more rock and breaking up more ore to be gathered and hauled up and processed and turned into money. It happened a couple times a day on every level they were working, which at the moment was just Four and Five.

The dust collected in the oil on the gears of the hoist and added some gum to the yuck that was already built up on the cable spool and spread through the lift house. It got into Billy Ray's nose and tickled there until he sneezed and had to wipe his nose and his eyes both. It happened regular as a clock. Somebody thousands of feet down would fire a charge and Billy Ray would have to sneeze. Sometimes he thought it was such a habit that come the Fourth of July when people set off firecrackers he would start sneezing as an automatic response to the little bitty charges.

The sneezing had his eyes watering, so he wiped at them again and leaned forward to listen as somebody down below dinged on the bell cord. They wanted the bucket on Five Level. Billy Ray checked his cable, shifted the levers, and dropped the bucket expertly to just where it had to be.

He never said anything about it as the boys who worked underground would only tease him if they knew, but he was proud of being able to put that bucket just where it had to be. And it was a half mile down and 'way out of sight.

He let the cable out fast, slowed at the last moment, and brought the thing to a bouncing stop spot on the money. There wasn't a better hoist operator anywhere on the mountain. Billy Ray believed that.

There was a wait while the bucket was loaded, then the bell jangled again and he brought it all the way up.

Nobody came up with it, just the ore

cart, so he had to call a couple boys from the crusher to come wrestle the cart off the bucket and on the tracks. They emptied the ore — already separated as best the muckers could tell to get rid of the trash rock — into the chute and returned the cart to the bucket.

It occurred to Billy Ray sometimes that there was probably an awful lot of good ore that was dumped into the trash heaps down below. Not that he was ever likely to go down and look for it. Huh uh. That was an underground job, and he knew better than to think a man could breathe easy down there. But likely those boys missed an awful lot of good ore when they did that first separating. The management liked for the muckers, who had to have plenty of muscle but not necessarily anything else for their jobs, like brains for instance, to cull out as much trash rock as they could and save the time and trouble of hauling it to the surface. So what they would do would be to put the ore-bearing rock into the carts and dump the rest of it wherever was handy, mostly into abandoned stopes or side tunnels where it would be out of the way. It made for a more efficient operation. But Billy Ray guessed the muckers missed some pretty good ore when they were doing their separating. He sometimes wondered just how much perfectly good gold was left laying there unclaimed.

"Clear," one of the boys from the crusher called. He banged the gate shut and latched it, and Billy Ray sent the now-empty cart back down to Five Level so they could fill it again with metal-bearing rock.

The hoist and bucket ran day and night, taking stiffs up and down, bringing ore up and taking tools and blasting supplies down. The rig ran as regular as a railroad watch, thank goodness. It was the only way in or out of those tunnels.

Billy Ray remembered one time, not too long after he started, when the operator — on the other shift, thank goodness — tried to force a lever without the clutch and stripped a gear on the donkey. They'd been working Two and Three then and just developing Four. The bucket got stuck just below the entrance to Three Level, and the whole outfit had to shut down until they could get a new gear shipped in, and that had taken two days. The off-shift boys had thought it something of a holiday, but it hadn't been so dang funny for the crews that were working deep at the time. Without the bucket the only way up was to climb the timbers in the shaft, with no ladder, just an occasional spike to step on. Two of the boys had refused to do it and had spent the whole time down below until the gear was replaced.

So Billy Ray considered himself an essential part of this operation, whether anybody else appreciated that or not.

The whistle for end of shift blew, and Billy Ray passed the word along on his bell cord. The bucket was already at Five, which would be the first crew up as they were working the deepest, so that was convenient. He hadn't long to wait before they signaled they were ready, and he brought them up. Slower than usual this time as he was for the moment aware of his responsibilities.

He let them off and gave the signal he was lowering — it wouldn't do to have some fool loafing at the edge with his legs hanging over and get the bucket cage dumped onto them — and let it down.

The Four Level crew came up owl-eyed from the dust that caked on them and with their lamps still burning. Tommy was among them but didn't so much as look in Billy Ray's direction again. He was getting to be more and more standoffish lately. Jealous was the way Billy Ray figured it, although he was sure willing to share his salvation and wouldn't quit trying to explain that to Tommy no matter what the fool went and did.

Rick Price, though, took off his hat and blew his lamp out and came over to Billy Ray's chair. "You going to town tonight?"

Billy Ray shrugged. "Haven't decided yet exactly. Why?"

"I was thinking. If you were going down, that is. I was thinking you could pick something up for me at the store."

"In that case I reckon I can go. What d'you need?"

Price gave him a funny kind of look for a moment. "You wouldn't mind doing that?"

"Naw. I've got things I can do there anyhow. Visit with some folks I need to see. No reason why I shouldn't make it tonight an' pick up your stuff too."

"You sure have changed, Billy Ray."

Billy Ray grinned at him. "Dang right I have. You want me to tell you why? 'Cause it's the Lord's doings, not mine."

Price glanced around, like he was checking to see that nobody was listening. The other boys were already filing down the stairs with their coats unbuttoned and lamps in their hands, fixing to get cleaned up and go eat.

"Maybe, uh, maybe I would wanta sit down and have a talk with you. You know. About that."

Billy Ray's grin got wider.

"But you ought to know, man, I done some powerful sinning in my time." He sounded rather proud of the depths of his sins.

"That's the neat thing about it, Rick. He already knows all that. An' while I can't say that He don't care, He's willing to wipe all that off the book, see. Just plain ol' forget about it like it never even happened. That's what this salvation stuff is all about. But we'll talk about that later. Let me get finished up here. When I get back from town we'll sit down an' talk about it."

"Yeah, uh." A bit of weak, tentative smile tugged briefly at the corners of Price's mouth. "We'll do that, Billy Ray."

"Good."

Price trailed the other boys down the ladder, and Billy Ray went back to his final chores of the shift. Already the second-shift crews were coming up the stairs, but the relief hoist operator wasn't up yet. The fellow was often late, but Billy Ray didn't get peeved about that lately the way he used to. Not that peeved was the way he would have put it then, but that was the idea.

He gave the second-shift foreman a greeting and told the man to go ahead and load his boys on the bucket. There wasn't any need for them to hang around waiting for Wally to get here.

Billy Ray was whistling softly under his breath, already looking forward to having that talk with Rick Price.

It occurred to him that Rick never said what he needed from town. Billy Ray would have to ask before he went.

Chapter 26

"What's your sermon on today, Billy Ray?" Price asked. Rick was walking down to services with him. It was even his own idea. Billy Ray had been wanting to ask him, but Rick came up with it on his own. That made Billy Ray feel pretty good, one of the boys from the Chagra No. 1 wanting to come to services.

"Ah, I don't give sermons, Rick. Takes a preacher to do that, and we don't have a real preacher. I just kinda talk some about the stuff I've been reading and thinking and, well, kinda feeling. You know."

"You're pretty sure about all this stuff, huh?"

"Heck, yes. It's right there in the book like I showed you, isn't it?"

"Yeah."

"All right then." They were running just a little bit later than usual. Billy Ray had cut himself shaving this morning and had a heckuva time getting the cut to quit bleeding. He'd finally had to find a dab of spider web — not so hard to do in most any corner of the bunkhouse — and press that over the slice so it would stop up.

There were already folks waiting on the open ground when they arrived. More folks even than last Sunday. Some of them had brought wooden folding chairs from someplace, and several different couples had blankets spread out on the ground.

Billy Ray counted. There were fifteen ladies and eleven husbands in the bunch. Lem Murphy was already there but without his friends this morning. And those two big fellows who never said anything or participated in anything but just stood at the back of the pack and stared at everybody, Billy Ray in particular. He noticed that the rich-looking men weren't there, but maybe they would still come along.

And of course there was Rick Price down from the Chagra with him. He felt like that was a real breakthrough. The very first of the boys to come and take salvation serious. He felt good about that.

Rick got to looking shy when they approached the rest of the people. He dropped back and stood near the big fellows, across on the other side of things from Murphy. Billy Ray went on by himself to the front. The folks saw him and the talking quieted down.

Mrs. Small and her ladies' choir told their husbands where to stay, and Harry Small stood behind them with the concertina. Billy Ray couldn't see anybody else coming down the road, so it was time to begin.

"Good morning. The Lord's given us a nice one today, ain't He? What we're gonna do here this morning is to pray some and sing some and then I'll tell you about what I been reading in Mark. I got through Matthew this week and got a start on Mark, you see. And there's some really interesting stuff in there, like about how we oughta act toward one another. That part comes from where Jesus is tellin' the crowds how they're all family, like. Like if they wanta follow the Lord, they got to stay straight with each other. So we'll talk some about that. First, though, I been looking forward to hearing the way these ladies sing, so I'll turn it over to Sister Melba Small an' let her tell you what they're going to do."

Billy Ray took a couple steps back, and Mrs. Small took a step forward. It surprised him when he thought about it, but this morning he wasn't scared so bad as he was to start with.

He hadn't been particularly last Sunday either, but he'd thought that was just because he was too busy then to think about it. But this week he had already worked it out with Miss Hattie to meet him after, and he wasn't scared again. Just a little bit, maybe, but not enough to fret about.

The truth was that he was enjoying this more and more.

He looked past Mrs. Small toward where Rick was standing and decided he'd better give a bit of a refresher about first being saved, too, though the ladies and at least some of their menfolk already had been. Rick hadn't been yet.

Later, at the very end of the service when Mrs. Small and the ladies were singing "Just As I Am" the most amazing dang thing happened.

Billy Ray was looking right straight at Rick Price when it happened, and for a minute or so there he couldn't hardly believe it. But he did. It took him right smack back to that time when Brother Greer had been here and Billy Ray got saved.

Rick was standing there looking kind of solemn and maybe worried about something. Then his expression changed. His jaw took on a stubborn set, and he shook his head like he was saying no to something. And then it was just like something inside him melted, and Rick Price began to bawl. Right out loud, standing there on the bare ground, with nobody but the two stone-faced big fellows close to him. He commenced to sob and shake and began walking forward.

Billy Ray ran forward and grabbed him and hugged him, and a couple of the ladies who weren't singing joined around them, and pretty soon everybody was crying, and one of the ladies was shouting "Glory" and "Hallelujah" and "Praise God," and some of the rest of them joined in, and Billy Ray was weeping so hard that he couldn't hardly see.

But he couldn't think of a time in his whole dang life when he'd ever been any happier or even come close to it.

Chapter 27

Billy Ray stood up, nearly as wet as Rick Price was, and helped Price to his feet. Rick was sopping wet from toes to hair tips, had to be every bit as cold as Billy Ray was but was grinning so wide and had been for so long that his jaw had to be aching from it. Billy Ray took him by the elbow and led him out of the water to dry ground.

"I didn't remember the words so good," Billy Ray apologized to all of them.

"Doesn't matter, Brother Halstad," Mrs. Kuntz said. "The Lord remembers them well enough."

"Yes, ma'am." Billy Ray made a mental note to go back through and re-read that part, though. He'd never baptized anybody before. He wanted to be able to do it right next time.

Nearly everybody was there on the creek bank watching and grinning. Everybody, he thought, except the two big fellows who'd slipped off when the rest of them headed down toward the creek. Even Murphy had come, which surprised Billy Ray.

"We'll have to get you up to the bunk-house so you can dry off before you catch your death," Billy Ray told Price.

"You will do no such thing, Brother Halstad," Mrs. Kuntz said. "That is much too far to walk in wet clothing. The young man will come to our house to dry off. You come too. You can both take dinner with us." Her husband, Janus, was listening but didn't offer any objection.

Price looked like he was just about knocked off his feet by the offer. And no wonder. Folks from the decent end of Blue Gorge didn't generally talk to a working stiff except to sell him something. Now here were the Kuntzes inviting him and Billy Ray home to dinner.

"Thanks, but you take Rick and go ahead. I made plans for this afternoon, and it wouldn't be right to break them."

"If you are sure, Brother Halstad?"

"Yes, ma'am. Sure do thank you, though."

The crowd broke up, everybody looking nearly as pleased with the events as Rick Price was, and Billy Ray put his shoes back on. He'd taken them off and left them on the bank when he went into the creek to baptize Rick, but he might as well have left them on. His socks and pant legs were running so much water that the shoes would get soaked anyhow.

"Well, reverend, I think you should be pleased with yourself today." It was Murphy, who had hung back when the rest of them left.

"What do you mean, Mr. Murphy?" Billy Ray thought about trying to correct the man once more about not being a reverend, but Murphy was one of those people who only listened when he wanted to. And that didn't seem to be often.

"You saved a soul today, didn't you?"

"No, sir. I just had some fun and got a little wet. The Lord does all the soul saving, not me."

Murphy seemed to find that funny, so he obviously didn't get the point.

"I need to talk with you again," the little man said.

"I'm busy this afternoon," Billy Ray said politely.

"We need your help, reverend. We want you on our side."

"Look, Mr. Murphy, for one thing I ain't no reverend. I'm just another guy. So I wish you'd quit calling me that. It makes me uncomfortable, like maybe people think I'm making more of myself than I am. For another thing, I don't wanta get mixed into something where I don't belong. I don't really care what you and the mine bosses work out. I'm more interested in a bigger boss than that. Okay?" He knelt and began tying his shoelaces. They were wet and limp already and difficult to handle.

"You don't care if you get a raise or not?"

"No, I don't." Billy Ray blinked and thought about what he'd just said. The funny thing was that it was true. He really didn't. He had not realized that until the words were already out of his mouth, but he truly didn't care about his pay envelope now. There were other things of much greater interest, and what had happened here this morning was one of them.

Murphy chuckled. "I thought preachers weren't supposed to lie."

"I'm not a preacher," Billy Ray said. He let it go at that, not caring enough to argue the point with Murphy.

"Have you read that literature I gave you?"

"Nope." He finished tying his shoes and stood, his pant legs clinging to him. The dry mountain air would take care of that soon enough, though. And he hadn't been quite as wet as Price after the dunking.

"You should," Murphy insisted. "There is a lot to be said for the union movement."

"Well, I haven't read it. Likely won't. I've been paying attention since you started this nonsense, Murphy. About unions, I mean. What I hear is that unions are a real fine idea. Really fine. But I don't hear that about your Mr. Haywood and the whatchamacallit he runs. If I was going to say anything about unions, which I ain't since that business belongs to Caesar an' not to the Lord, I still wouldn't say anything good about your crowd." Billy Ray picked up his coat and Bible and started up the bank.

"Who the hell is this Caesar you're talking about?" Murphy demanded. The little man sounded hot.

Billy Ray laughed at him. "Management, not labor. But you don't have to worry about him. He's an old-timer."

"Are you telling me you're siding with management, damn you?"

Billy Ray laughed again. "Mr. Murphy, the only thing I'm telling you right now is that I got an engagement this afternoon that I don't wanta be late for. Okay?"

"Don't you get to be thinking you're too big to be taken down a peg, Mister Reverend Halstad," Murphy snapped toward Billy Ray's back.

Billy Ray did hear him, even if he didn't bother to acknowledge it. Too big, huh. Shee-oot. That Murphy was a case. Before he had gone a dozen paces, though, Mr. Murphy was far from Billy Ray's thoughts.

Chapter 28

Tuesday morning Billy Ray walked up through the snowshed to the mine with Rick Price, trying to steal a little time to go through again the discussion they'd been having last night. Rick was still pleased to have been saved but getting a little scared of it now that it had gone and happened.

"The thing is," he was saying in the changing room while he was getting his cap and making sure his lamp was filled. "The thing is, dang it, I don't know if I'm man enough for this. You got to give up an awful lot."

Tommy Johnson and some of the other boys were in there putting on their canvas coats too and getting ready for the shift. The other boys were wanting to snicker. Tommy just looked uneasy. Billy Ray tried to make like he wasn't aware of them, but he was.

"That's the whole point I been trying to

make with you, Rick," he said, just loud enough that those other boys could hear too. "You don't *give up* nothing. What you do is to get and not give up. Why, the Boss already knows all the things you done. That didn't keep Him from giving you the gift in the first place. And He don't lie nor take gifts back. What you got is yours to keep. Right on till after you die. So if you really *want* to go on with all the crap you useta do, why, you just have at it. Won't mean a lick to bein' saved. The point is, once you got the glory, Rick, I just can't believe you want to sin. Not deliberate. 'Cause Jesus suffered on that cross for every sin you done and every one you will do, an' I don't think you'll wanta do anything to make Him have suffered anymore than you can help. At least that's the way I see it."

Rick grunted and headed up the stairs with Billy Ray following close behind. There wasn't time to talk about it anymore, but he could chew on it through the day. Billy Ray wasn't really worried about him. And behind them the other boys had gotten their ears full too, whether they wanted to or not.

The shift foreman was already up at the top by the hoist, waiting for the crews to assemble. Billy Ray took over from the relief operator and took a quick look at the cable and his hoist gears to make sure everything was as it should be. When he was satisfied he gave the foreman the nod, and the man started putting crews onto the bucket and telling Billy Ray where to put them. Which was really unnecessary as Billy Ray knew where they were going as well as the foreman did, but that was the way they liked to do things.

Billy Ray shuttled them down, a bucket load at a time, until every last man was in position far below inside the mountain. Then he brought the bucket back up, set the safety brake so nothing exciting was likely to happen, and reached for his oilcan.

"Halstad."

"Yeah?"

"You're wanted down at the assayer's office."

"Me?"

"They said Halstad. That sounds like you."

Billy Ray shrugged. He couldn't see any reason why Barney Craddock would want to see him. But then the best way to find out would be to go down and see. If a boss said to go it was up to him to do it.

"What about the hoist?" he asked as he headed for the stairs. "Do they need anything down below and I'm not here . . ."

"I'll watch it while you're gone."

"Okay." Better to hurry, though, he thought. He didn't want to be away from his station too long.

He hurried down the levels to the bottom and stopped outside Barney's door, which was closed. That was unusual, but Barney had the right to some privacy if he wanted, Billy Ray guessed. Billy Ray cleared his throat, feeling as much nervous as curious now that he was down here, and knocked.

"Come." That hadn't been Barney's voice. He was sure of that.

He opened the door and faced two of the big bosses, Mr. Valdura the general manager and Mr. Fischer, whose title Billy Ray didn't know but who was high enough up that he worked in the office down in town instead of having to come up the path to the mine every day. There was no sign at all of Barney Craddock except for the litter on his desk.

"Excuse me," Billy Ray said quickly. "I didn't . . . I mean I thought I was supposed to see Barney. I didn't mean to disturb you gentlemen." He started to back out and pull the door closed behind him.

"Wait." It was Mr. Fischer who said that. "You're Halstad?"

"Yes, sir."

"Come inside and shut the door."

"Yes, sir." Billy Ray was really nervous now. He tried to think of what he might have done, any way he could have messed up with the hoist . . . He could not come up with anything.

"You are a damned disloyal employee, Halstad," Fischer said coldly.

"Sir?"

"Even after you were warned, you persisted in consorting with the Wobblies."

"But . . ."

"I want no lip from your kind, Halstad. Believe me, my personal preference would be to give you a sound thrashing. A sound thrashing, sir."

Billy Ray's eyes got wide. And not only with disbelief over what Mr. Fischer was saying about him and that dumb Murphy fellow, which was what this had to be about. Thrash him? Mr. Fischer was a head shorter and twenty years older than Billy Ray. Thrash him? Shee-oot. That'd be the day.

"If you'll let me explain . . ."

"None of your lies, man," Fischer butted

in again. "Here." He reached inside a coat pocket, pulled out a little brown envelope like pay came in, and shoved it at Billy Ray.

Billy Ray reached out and took the thing without thinking about it. Right now he *couldn't* think about much anyhow.

"We no longer require your services, Halstad. Clear out. Now."

Billy Ray turned and stumbled away in a state of shocked confusion.

Chapter 29

Billy Ray blinked. He was at the top of the long chain of stairs. Up by the hoist. He didn't know why he had come up here again. Except habit. This was where he worked. This was what he did. Of course he would come up to the hoist. Except that he didn't work here anymore, and the hoist was no longer his to be responsible for and to operate.

The foreman was sitting in Billy Ray's chair — in the hoist operator's chair — with his feet propped up on a grease bucket and a pipe in his hand. He was filling the pipe with slow, affectionate care. "That didn't take long." He started to give the place back to Billy Ray.

Billy Ray blinked again and stared stupidly down toward the pay envelope he was still holding. He could feel that it contained a few coins. "Stay . . . uh . . . I just came up to get my dinner box."

"What the hell's that supposed to mean?"

"I been fired." Billy Ray's voice was dull. That was all right. His brain felt dull too. "I never been fired from any job in my life before," he said.

"Damn." The foreman made a face and shoved the partially filled pipe back into his pocket. "What am I supposed to do for a hoist operator now?"

Billy Ray shrugged. He picked up the boxed lunch that the boardinghouse had ready for each of them in the mornings and looked around. There was nothing else of his here. Nothing that he should take away with him. That was hard to believe, that there was no personal mark of his anywhere in the hoist shed, but it was true. There was nothing.

"I'm sorry about that, Halstad," the foreman said. By then Billy Ray was shuffling toward the stairs. He did not respond to the foreman's voice.

He tried to think this through, but it was not easy. He was not sure what he ought to be thinking about or what he ought to be doing. He did not know where to go.

Six days a week, seven back when things were busier and the mine producing more, a man worked. That was all there was to it. A man worked.

So what did a man do when he didn't have work?

Billy Ray did not know.

He went down the stairs again and out past Barney Craddock's office. The door was open now and Barney was inside. Barney did not look up when Billy Ray passed, and Billy Ray did not give the chemist his usual cheerful wave in passing. Barney probably knew, probably would be embarrassed for him. Maybe even ashamed to be seen having Billy Ray wave at him. So Billy Ray went on past and out through the changing room and back through the snowshed to the back of the bunkhouse.

The bunkhouse seemed awfully quiet and empty. The cooks would have been up early, way before dawn, to get the breakfast ready and the lunches packed, and now they would likely be getting in some extra sleep before they had to start cooking supper for the end of the shift.

Up on the top floor the night shift boys were moving around, getting ready to go to bed. Billy Ray did not want to see any of them. One look at him, idling around in the bunkhouse in broad daylight, and they would know what had happened. He didn't want to talk to any of them.

Not to anybody else either, for that matter.

Right now he guessed he just wanted to be alone.

He wondered for a moment if he was supposed to go up now and clean out his things and get out of the bunkhouse too.

That could wait, he decided. He was paid up for the rest of this week. So he didn't have to be in that much of a hurry to clear out. Or did he? The boarding-house belonged to the mine company too. Maybe when they fired someone they kicked him out of his bunk too. Except that he was paid up in advance.

He checked inside the envelope Mr. Fischer had given him. It held six dollars. Pay for yesterday and today but no refund on the board bill he had already paid from last week's envelope. So probably he didn't have to move his things out just yet.

They probably thought they were being generous to pay him a full wage for today though he hadn't put in a full shift of work.

Jesus!

That short appeal helped to settle him. A little anyway.

He dropped the six dollars into his pocket and tucked the dinner box under his arm and hurried on through the bunkhouse and out the front before anyone might see him. For some reason he really did not want anyone to see him there.

He started down the path, still moving without reason, still feeling dumb and numb and unsure about things. He found himself walking faster and faster and then breaking into a run down the path.

It was like if he moved fast enough and far enough the thinking wouldn't catch up with him. Like if he could just get out in front of it all, why, it would be all right again, and tomorrow morning, why, he could climb back up the stairs and sit down at the hoist and everything would be just like it had been.

Except that that wouldn't be. He knew it wouldn't be, but he refused to think about that for right now.

He ran like hell down the path to Blue Gorge.

Chapter 30

He sat beside the creek with his knees drawn up tight against his chest and his forehead resting on them. He didn't want to look at anything. The sound of the creek was loud. Soothing, sort of. It was something to listen to that didn't have to be thought about or answered. It was just there.

It was still early. Too early by a little for the town to be active. Which seemed hard to believe considering everything that had already happened this morning, but was a blessing because it meant he didn't have to face anyone yet.

He didn't know why he had come here. He had just done it without thinking. This was about the only place he knew around Blue Gorge where he could just get away from people and be by himself for a while. He had not consciously thought that out, but it was so.

He was still in something of a state of

shock. He did not know how to cope with this one. He tried praying but did not want to concentrate on that either. Not even on that. That worried him, but he did not argue with it. Later. He could pray later. Right now he wished he could just . . . sleep, go numb, get drunk, and forget about this whole bullshit thing. He didn't know what he wanted to do. He wanted to do something. More than that, though, he wanted to do nothing.

Something touched him on the shoulder, and he jumped so hard he almost threw his neck out of joint.

"Billy Ray."

It was Miss Hattie. Standing over him, smiling, looking for all the world like there was nothing wrong and this was just another perfectly ordinary morning. But then she wouldn't have any way to know that it wasn't.

She looked at him and the smile disappeared and was replaced by something more serious. "Are you all right, Billy Ray?" She sat down beside him, having to shift the box lunch to make room close to him.

"No," he blurted. He did not want to see anybody or talk to anybody or have anybody know what had gone and happened to him this morning, but even while he was thinking that and thinking that he should tell her . . . ask her . . . to go away he was already telling her all about it. Everything. And Hattie was listening, looking solemn and concerned, nodding now and then, reaching over every once in a while to pat his wrist or touch his arm. Billy Ray thought he was going to cry. He was *not* going to cry, dammit. He was not.

He started to cry a little and turned his head away so that she wouldn't see, but he kept on talking. Now that he had started it was like he couldn't stop talking if he wanted to. Hattie patted his arm again.

"I tried to tell them," he was saying. "I tried to tell them that it was that damned Murphy. I'll just bet it was that Murphy deliberately spreading rumors about me, stories about me fixing to speak in favor of the unions. He'd do that sort of thing. Just because I refused to speak for his union. He as much as said he'd do something of the like. And I ain't quite so dumb as they think. The union folks and the management folks too, they've both been there spying Sunday mornings during services. Took me a while to realize that, but that's who some of those people were. Both sides afraid I was gonna say something that would favor the other. Dammit, Hattie, I don't care about none of that. I've tried to tell 'em so, too. I just stood up and said what salvation is about. I don't care about any da . . . dang union position or management one neither. I tried to tell Murphy that, but it wouldn't do. He wouldn't listen. Neither would Mr. Fischer. And that Mr. Valdura, standing there and not saying a word and having Mr. Fischer do the dirty work for him. But neither one of them wanted to listen to anything I might say, not a lick more than Murphy would."

That was true, Billy Ray figured. That had to be what this was all about. Though he hadn't realized any of that until he heard himself tell Miss Hattie about it.

He just hadn't thought it out until now. Thought it out? Shee-oot, he hadn't thought about any-dang-thing since Fischer told him he was fired.

Billy Ray rubbed the back of his hand over his eyes and turned to look at Miss Hattie. "I'll tell you something else," he said in a low, serious voice. "That damn Murphy thinks he'll have me whipped once he has me fired. Well, he got me fired, I reckon. No help for that. An' I sure don't know what he's afraid of anyhow. I'm just a working stiff . . ." He smiled, a little, and amended that to "Former workin' stiff, anyhow. So I don't know what he's so worried about what I say or do anyhow. But I'll tell you something, Miss Hattie. Him, anybody, they can do whatever they want to dumb ol' Billy Ray Halstad. But there ain't anybody, not here, not anyplace, that can shut up the Lord. Huh uh. Not anybody can do that. So if they think they can stop me or anybody else from speaking out just because of getting fired, why, they got themselves another think t'do on that one."

He sat up straighter and was able to actually grin at Miss Hattie. "Why, this being fired, it's terrible. Awfullest thing that ever happened to me. Or maybe it ain't. Why, it just could be that this here is part o' the Lord's plan of things. I told the Boss He could do whatever He wanted with me. Maybe this is it. Maybe He wants me to put more time into telling people about Him instead of running miners up an' down a hole in the ground. That could be, don't you think?"

"I wouldn't know about anything like that, Billy Ray."

"Well, I'm just guessing myself. But I reckon it could be." He grinned again. "I expect I can go ahead that way. Does He want anything different, why, He can slap me down an' tell me so."

"All right. If that's what you want."

"Hey, it isn't what I want that counts. It's whatever the Lord wants me to do that matters. I sure ain't going to tell Him He's wrong."

Billy Ray was feeling dang good now. In spite of everything that had just happened, why, he was feeling dang good.

He reached across Miss Hattie for the box lunch. "I don't know about you, but I'm hungry all of a sudden. Let's see what we have here."

"All right." She smiled at him, and he felt better than ever.

Chapter 31

A man is supposed to work, and doing what the Lord wants is no excuse for laziness the way Billy Ray figured it.

So he tramped up and down the paths. Not up toward the Chagra No. 1, of course, nor to the Chagra No. 4 which was a mile or so above Blue Gorge at the head of one of the side canyons, but to just about every other company he could find or think of.

Nobody wanted another hoist operator. Nor for that matter any other kind of aboveground worker. Which was kind of strange. Generally speaking there was always work available for a man willing to do it, but not right now, it seemed.

Finally Mr. Kuntz, who was the chief geologist at the Margaret Mae, took him aside and clued him in.

Mr. Kuntz caught him just as he was leaving the place after getting another turndown. He took Billy Ray by the arm and took him aside into Mr. Kuntz's private office, which was about as full of charts and papers and core samples as Barney Craddock's little office had been full of ore samples and crucibles and such. Mr. Kuntz looked embarrassed.

"I don't know how to tell you this, Brother Halstad, but . . . the truth is that, I mean I know you are a reverend and a good man . . . but the truth is, you see, that you've been blacklisted."

Billy Ray was so surprised that he didn't even think to remind Mr. Kuntz that he was no reverend and shouldn't be taken for one. "Blacklisted. What's that?"

Mr. Kuntz wouldn't meet his eyes but turned his head away. "I am sorry, Reverend Halstad. And please don't tell anyone that I've told this to you. My employers would not understand, and my missus would never be able to understand why I can't do anything about it, although I can't. Believe me, I would if I could. But the simple truth is that as long as you are on the blacklist, Reverend Halstad, there isn't a company on this mountain that would hire you."

Billy Ray puffed his cheeks out and slowly exhaled, taking some time to work this through. "Mr. Valdura, huh?"

Kuntz did not answer.

"Thank you for telling me, Mr. Kuntz. It saves me a lot of trouble."

"I am truly sorry, Reverend Halstad. Believe me when I say that. I am truly sorry."

"Aw, you didn't do it."

"If I could do anything, anything to change it, I would."

Billy Ray smiled at him. "No need for you to apologize, Mr. Kuntz. But please don't call me Reverend no more. I'm just a guy. Okay?"

Kuntz's expression was uncomprehending, but he nodded agreement, probably out of a willingness to do anything he could to make Billy Ray feel better than from any understanding of the request.

"Is your wife feeling well still?" Billy Ray asked.

"Off and on," Kuntz said. "She was feeling a little poorly this morning."

"Would you mind if I called on her then to see if I can help? I could wait until this evening and come by then."

"Wouldn't mind at all," Kuntz assured him. "And you needn't wait until evening. She would appreciate your interest, so stop by whenever it is convenient for you, Brother Halstad."

Billy Ray grinned at the man. "Most any time of day suits me now. So I'll stop in directly an' have a word of prayer with her. I got to warn you, though. We'll likely do some praying for your soul too, Mr. Kuntz. I don't believe you've been saved yet."

"No. But I have to admit that I like the things you've been saying, Reverend Halstad. You know the way it is for a man, and you talk so I can understand it."

"If you have any questions . . ."

Kuntz shook his head. "Not right now. But I might. Sometime. If I ever do . . ."

"If you ever do, sir, you just ask. I'll tell you as best I can, an' what I don't know — and there's aplenty that I don't know myself — but whatever I don't know, sir, the good Lord does. He'll set you straight if you just give Him a chance."

"You really believe that, don't you?"

"Yes, sir. I really do."

"Then maybe we should talk sometime."

"Any time at all, sir." Billy Ray laughed. "I sure don't have anything more pressing nowadays."

"Then good luck to you, Reverend Halstad."

Billy Ray gave Kuntz a thumbs-up sign as he headed for the door. "I don't need luck, Mr. Kuntz. I got something better."

Funny thing, he thought as he walked back down toward town. Finding out about the blacklist didn't bother him a bit. He began to whistle and to wonder if it was early enough that he might still catch Miss Hattie at the creek bank. He hadn't thought about that before the other day, but she didn't just come there Sunday mornings the way he'd been assuming since he was only down to see her there on Sundays. She found the time to go there most every morning. And that was kind of nice. He stepped up his pace a little and began to swing his arms in time to his whistling.

Chapter 32

"I couldn't pay you much."

"That's all right, sir. I don't need much."

"It's a poor job for . . . well, it is a poor job."

"I don't mind, sir."

"A dollar a day is all I can pay. And you could sleep in the back room if you like."

"That would be just fine, sir. And I'll do the best by you that I can."

"I never would have thought . . ." Doc Hoosier shook his head. "I mean, a reverend such as yourself . . ."

"Just Billy Ray, sir. And I thank you for the work."

"Then I'll show you where you can put your things," Billy Ray's new boss said.

The pay would not be much, but then the job would not be much either. Doc just expected him to keep the place swept out and more or less straightened up and now and then to help out with the heavy work of grinding chemicals with the mortar and pestle, which Doc said was becoming a chore for him at his age. Doc himself, of course, would do all the mixing and combining of the ingredients while Billy Ray ground them to a powder for him.

It was work, after all, and as for the pay being slim, well, Billy Ray did not need much to get along on. He still had pay left over from his time with the Chagra No. 1.

Better yet it would give him a place to stay. That had been bothering him some. He did not intend to leave Blue Gorge, by gum, but the thought of having to sleep in a packing crate, or worse, was unpleasant. A cot in the rear of Doc's store would suit him fine.

And best of all, Doc had already said he wouldn't mind if Billy Ray needed time away from the shop to go and call on folks or pray with them or attend to whatever their needs were.

"After all," Doc had said, "in a way you could say that we are both in the business of tending to people's needs. We just go about it in different ways, Reverend Halstad."

Which was nice except that everybody was insisting on calling him by that unearned title lately, and he couldn't seem to break them from it. It was positively embarrassing.

Billy Ray left the apothecary and started up the familiar path toward the bunkhouse.

At least at this time of day he would not have to run into any of the boys. That would have been a bit tough to take. But except for that, why, things were going along a lot better than he ever would have expected.

Chapter 33

There was a heckuva turnout for services Sunday morning. Thirty-four people by Billy Ray's count. Of course not quite all of them had come to hear the word. He knew that.

Aside from a couple kids who had come with their folks — which was nice as that was a first of sorts — there were some fellows who had just come to hear if Brother Billy Ray Halstad was going to be lambasting anybody.

That so-and-so Murphy didn't show up himself, but he sent his two friends along to listen and report back to him. Billy Ray still figured Murphy to be behind the rumors, probably figuring that if the company fired him Billy Ray would want to strike back at them by saying bad things about them during services. Which dang sure wasn't going to work, but Murphy would not know that.

And then there were the management hard cases, which is what Billy Ray figured those two big, quiet guys to be. They were there as usual. And there were a couple management-looking men there again too. Some of the same ones who'd been coming from the start and then had quit for a while.

So that meant that both sides had sent some people not to listen to the word but to listen and see if sides were being taken.

Billy Ray kind of grinned to himself over that. Let them come. They weren't going to hear what they were worried about, but they would dang sure get an earful about the Lord. That was what counted here.

He noticed that there were a fair number of stiffs in the crowd. Rick Price was down, of course. He was the only one Billy Ray recognized from the Chagra No. 1 although the short, dark-haired fellow with the bushy moustache standing next to Rick might have been a stiff from the night shift at the Chagra. Billy Ray was not sure about him.

Besides them, though, there were a number of other boys whose clothes gave them away as working men. Probably they had come to see what this bull was all about and whether this former stiff standing in front of them could hold his head up after getting fired. Fine. He was willing to show them. And to tell them something in the bargain. However they got dragged in was all right as long as they kept their ears open and listened. Billy Ray wasn't proud about how they came, just about what they heard.

The ladies of the choir were in fine voice, pleased to be singing to so many he thought, and they did a bang-up job with the hymns.

Billy Ray had thought about this morning all through the time since he got himself fired. It was a help that he'd had a lot more time for his reading this week, because what he needed was all the way over in Luke and he wouldn't have got to it if it was not for the extra time on his hands.

When the ladies got through with their opening hymns and it was time for Billy Ray to say something he thanked the choir and took a few steps forward.

For a minute or so he stood there, looking the folks in the eyes, one by one, and not for a minute backing off from Murphy's friends or from the company men.

He looked everybody over for that minute, then he paused and took a deep breath.

" 'Get thee behind me, Satan,' " he roared. No warning. He just cut loose with it as loud as he could holler. " 'For it is written, Thou shalt worship the Lord thy God, and him only shalt thou serve.' "

He let that part rip. Then in a quieter tone he added, "That there comes from Luke, folks. Fourth chapter o' Luke. And that is where ol' Satan took Jesus out to the wilderness and tried to tempt Him. Tried to get Him to roll over an' be a sinner from hunger an' from all the other temptations that man is heir to. But do you know what the Lord said? He said that bread don't matter. Worldly stuff don't matter. It's the word o' God an' *only* the word o' God that counts. And he told that old devil to go take a hike, because Jesus wasn't buying any of his bull. Well, boys, an' ladies, let me tell you something here. Jesus was right about that. This worldly stuff, who has what, who owns what, who does what, who wants what, none of that matters a lick or a spittle. I been finding out about that lately, and it's the natural truth."

He paused again and looked the crowd over. Right here was where they would be expecting him to go ahead and put the knock on somebody. Well, they could wait for that all they wanted, and all the better the closer they listened for it. That right there was all he intended to say on that particular subject, and the heck with the whole bunch of them.

"Let me tell you what else I found in Luke this week," he said, and went right on from there.

It wasn't, by golly, a bad old service, and long before it was over Billy Ray found that he was having fun with it, if for nothing else but to watch the expressions on the faces of Murphy's friends over on that side and on the management boys over on the other side and each of them waiting for him to cut loose and lay into them. They could wait, and they could listen. Billy Ray was enjoying himself now.

Chapter 34

This business of using a pestle was harder work than Billy Ray would have thought until he got to doing it. A fellow had to bear down hard, leaning down into it, and apply plenty of wrist and forearm to get Doc's lumps and seeds and rocks broken and finally powdered fine. It took a while. Billy Ray straightened for a moment, brushed a lock of hair back out of his eyes and shook a little to help untangle the kinks in his back. That wasn't getting it done, though, so he took only a bit of a rest and bent down to it again. He was trying to powder some hard, shiny chunks of alum, which Doc wanted for something or other — Billy Ray didn't pretend to understand what any of this stuff was for — and the alum not only looked like quartz rock it was every bit as hard as quartz. Seemed like it right now anyhow.

He prodded and ground and bore down the way Doc had showed him and was rewarded with the tiniest bit of progress.

There was a welcome interruption when the shop door opened and Mrs. Harmon came inside. Mrs. Harmon was one of the new members of the congregation — Billy Ray had started to think of the Sunday morning folks as a congregation lately, even though it wasn't like they had a regular church or a real preacher or anything — and he was hoping that she would be able to get her husband to coming too pretty soon.

He let go of the pestle and shoved the mortar aside with no reluctance at all and stood to greet the lady with a smile. "Good morning, Mrs. Harmon. Doc is in the back. Do you want me to call him for you?"

"No need, Reverend Halstad. I just need to buy one of these." She picked one of the bottles of patent medicines off a shelf and brought it to the counter.

"Yes, ma'am." Billy Ray accepted the coin she laid down and made change out of the cigar box. "You folks are well?"

"Passing fair, Reverend Halstad."

"If you need me to call . . ." he offered.

"Oh, I shouldn't think so. But I do hear that Mrs. Kuntz is ill again."

"I'll make it a point to stop over this evening then. Thank you for telling me."

Mrs. Harmon dropped her change and bottle of medication into her handbag. "Your coming to us has been such a blessing, Reverend Halstad. Such a blessing."

"That's very kind of you, Mrs. Harmon, but I keep trying to explain . . ."

"I know. I know. You tell us that every week. I still say it's a blessing."

"Yes, ma'am. But you know, I've been thinking. There are getting to be quite a lot of us now. Most enough, I should think, to ask a real reverend to come and minister to us. Time, maybe, for all of us to get together and talk about that. You know. Hire someone. If everybody is willing, that is. I've been thinking maybe we should talk about that come Sunday."

"You aren't thinking of leaving are you, Reverend Halstad?"

Billy Ray smiled at her. "No, ma'am, not at all. I'd be there in the front row, smack in the middle. There's a lot I got to learn yet."

Mrs. Harmon sniffed loudly. "We shall see, Reverend Halstad. Some of us have been talking, though."

"Yes, ma'am?"

"We can't count on fine weather every week. Some of us think we should look for a place to meet. Even build a church."

"Why, I think that would be an excellent idea, ma'am. 'Bout time this town had itself a real church. A real preacher too. There's a lot of work to be done here. A lot of work."

Mrs. Harmon sniffed again and sent a stern look up-gorge, right on through Doc Hoosier's walls and on toward the rowdy end of town where all the saloons and cribs were located. She didn't have to explain anything for Billy Ray to understand her meaning. The ladies of the congregation felt no charity toward the sporting girls who worked up at that end of town. "That lot needs to be cleaned out, Reverend Halstad. Fire and brimstone is what I say. Fire and brimstone."

"I kinda think the Lord would rather save 'em than burn 'em, ma'am. After all, we're all sinners. The difference is which sins, not whether we done any or not."

"There are degrees of sinning, Reverend Halstad," Mrs. Harmon said crossly.

"Yes, ma'am, so there are. An' one of the nice things about salvation is that the Lord forgives all of 'em. Darn good thing too or I wouldn't never have got saved."

Mrs. Harmon sniffed. It sounded just about as loud as a boar can snort. She turned away from the counter.

"If you or any of yours need me for anything, Mrs. Harmon, you be sure an' let me know."

She sailed out through the door without answering. Billy Ray was beginning to realize that some folks seemed to think they had exclusive rights to salvation. Like once they had theirs they had to start worrying that there wouldn't be enough to go around and they'd best protect it lest theirs get taken away and given to some lower class of sinner.

That was one thing Billy Ray figured he didn't have to worry about. There wasn't hardly any class of sinner lower than he'd been, so he was in no matter who was right about that.

He chuckled a little, thinking about the absurdity of that, and went back to powdering Doc's alum.

Chapter 35

They might not be able to count on fine, fair days every day, but this certainly was one. Billy Ray hoped it would be as fine for services tomorrow. Tonight, of course, they would be open late, mostly handing out bandages and poultices. And tomorrow afternoon Doc would be open to sell medications intended to ease sour stomachs and take the pounding out of aching heads.

There had been a time when Saturdays meant something special to him. Well, they still did. But for a different reason. Nowadays Saturdays were when he had to concentrate on getting his thoughts together for tomorrow's talking. He still couldn't think of it as preaching. Just talking.

"You have everything that I asked you for?" Doc said as he came into the front of the shop.

"It's all right there, labeled and everything."

"Good, Billy Ray. We'll be open late tonight, so if you want to take a little time for yourself now, you go right ahead and do it."

"Thanks, Doc." Hoosier was a good man to work for. He made it seem like they were working together. "I want to go and do some quiet reading. But I won't be late getting back."

"You go ahead, Billy Ray."

"Have you thought any more about coming to services tomorrow?"

"You know I got to have the shop open, Billy Ray."

"Not till noon, you don't."

"I'll think about it."

"You do that, Doc." Billy Ray was determined to get Doc to services. No hurry about it, though. Billy Ray was willing to wait until Doc was ready. Salvation wasn't something you could drag anyone into. They had to be willing. The Lord always was but not always His folks.

Billy Ray went into the back room where Doc had set a cot for him and a small trunk where he could keep his things. He got his Bible and left, stopped at Mercheson's for half a loaf of bread and a dollop of jam wrapped in a twist of oiled paper, and headed down toward the creek.

With the weather so fair it was more pleasant to do his reading down there when he could than inside the close confinement of Doc's little back room. He stifled a yawn and told himself he was going to have to watch himself this afternoon or he would end up lazing the day away instead of studying. And that wouldn't do. He had no idea what he would talk about tomorrow and had to come up with something pretty dang soon.

There was the usual bustle of activity on the street this afternoon as the better folks in town got all their shopping done before the day shifts at the mines turned loose and began to raise Cain. Saturday nights tended to be noisy, which Billy Ray had never noticed particularly before but did now.

"Afternoon, ma'am," he said to a woman he passed on the sidewalk. He did not know her but thought he had seen her before with Mrs. Horvath.

He smiled and spoke to two gentlemen coming out of Blue Gorge's stock brokerage, which was operated by a man who doubled as the town's only lawyer. Billy Ray did not actually know either of the gentlemen but he recognized one of them as being one of the management people who kept an ear on his talking. They smiled and spoke back to him.

He ambled on down the street toward the creek and the private spot where he sometimes met Miss Hattie and nowadays sometimes studied his Bible. He was reading in Acts now and was purely excited by the things he was finding there.

A lady was coming out of the mercantile down in the next block. She was too far away for him to be sure of who she was, but she looked familiar. Billy Ray got a smile all ready to give her.

He didn't, though.

The fine, lazy afternoon was stopped in its tracks by the screech of a steam whistle high on the mountain.

This wasn't the time of day for a shift change. Not for an hour or better yet.

And the whistle didn't just blow and fall silent. It screeched and screeched and went on howling, whoever was pulling the chain letting up for barely a moment before he yanked on it again.

"Oh Lord," Billy Ray whispered as he ran to the mouth of the next cross street and turned to look, seeing if he could spot where the whistle was. All up and down the street other men were doing the same, and the women on the street stopped where they were looking confused and worried.

"Chagra One," someone shouted just as Billy Ray was reaching the same conclusion. "There's trouble at the Chagra One."

The emergency whistle continued to squawl, but up and down the valley there was an ominous silence as stamp mills at the other mines quit their incessant pounding. Other whistles at other mines hooted flurries of quick call-up signals.

"Jesus," Billy Ray mumbled.

Then he was running, racing for the narrow path he had known so well. His heart was pounding even harder than his feet as he ran up the path.

Above him at the Chagra the steam whistle continued to blow.

"Jesus, help them," Billy Ray prayed as he ran.

Chapter 36

Billy Ray grabbed a cap and lamp off the pegs in the changing room and raced on through the familiar mill, past Barney's office and up the stairs, past the chutes and float tanks and crushers and on up to the hoist shed at the very top.

The place was filled solid with grim-faced men from the night shift. Billy Ray's replacement on the hoist was a young fellow who had been on the night shift before. Danny something-or-other. Billy Ray could not remember his name now.

The steam donkey was working, spooling the bucket up from someplace down below. Billy Ray held his Bible over his chest like a shield against the news from underground and edged forward.

There was a dry smell of rock dust in the air inside the shed. It seemed much heavier than he ever remembered it being, but that could have been a matter of him forgetting and not really anything new.

The top of the bucket cage reached the top landing, and Danny brought it to a stop. Artie Alphabet was in the bucket, holding onto a man named Rolf who was holding his right arm in his left hand and looking haggard and in pain. Both men were covered solid with rock dust so that clothes and skin and everything except their eyes and lips were caked to a uniform color.

"The son'bitch is gone, boys," Artie shouted. "Four Level, she's gone. Fell all in, boys."

There was a buzz of low conversation through the relief men, and a couple of them helped Rolf out of the bucket.

"How many you got room for down there, Artie?" someone called.

"Da Five Level crew is dere already, boys. Pullin' rock from da cave-in. Damn t'ing fell in dis sida da stopes. We got to pull da rock all da way to da shaft an' dump 'er dere."

It was a bad one, then. Any cave-in was a bad one, but this one had happened close to the start of the Four Level tunnel. There would be no telling how far back it extended. It could be an impossible amount of work involved to reach the Four Level crew trapped behind it. If any of them were still alive to reach. On the other hand, with so much tunnel and so many working stopes behind the cave-in, there would be a fair amount of air trapped behind the rock with those boys. If they could be reached at all, there was at least a fair chance that they could remain alive until the emergency crews reached them.

Billy Ray could hear more heavy footfalls on the bank of stairs leading down from the hoist shed. That would be stiffs coming on the run from the nearby mines. And boys from the distant holes would not be far behind them. There would not be a stiff in the gorge who would be willing to rest until the boys down below were reached.

Or given up.

Billy Ray shuddered. There was nothing he could think of that would be worse, nothing that could possibly be close to being half as bad, as being trapped underneath those countless tons of cold, gray rock. Trapped there in total darkness. Still alive but dying bit by bit from lack of air. From exposure to the water that seeped into the tunnels through the rock walls. From the sheer terror of it.

"You down there, Lord?" Billy Ray asked. "That's where You're needed right now. Get down there, please, an' help those boys."

The daytime Four Level crew. Jesus! That would be Rick Price. And Tommy Johnson. Both of them would be behind the cave-in.

"You got room for any more of us?" one of the night shift boys asked.

"Ayuh. One, two buckets. Foreman says send boys down. Da day crew be pretty tired already, you know. We replace dem soon."

Every man in the shed tried to surge forward to the bucket, anxious to be down there doing something to help.

Billy Ray found himself among them. He was petrified of being underground. Even without the threat of cave-in just being below ground scared him. And now there was a strong likelihood that more caving could take place. The tunnel roof was already weakened. Every man among them knew that the probability of more caving was high now that one section of the roof had given way. But dammit, that was where he was needed.

The bucket was swaying and bouncing on the cable eyebolt as boys from the night shift tried to crowd aboard it.

Billy Ray reached the edge of the landing

236

and tried not to think about the thousands of feet of straight drop that gaped practically under his toes. He grabbed Artie by the sleeve.

"Billy Ray. What th' hell are you doin' here?"

"I got to be there, Artie. I got to get down there and help."

"But you don't . . ."

"I got to, Artie."

"All right." Artie nodded and poked one of the night shift boys in the ribs. "You take da next bucket, okay? Preacher, he got to be there to give da last rites, maybe."

The stiff from the night shift blinked and looked like he wanted to argue it, but Artie gave him a shove and got him muscled out of the bucket so there was room for Billy Ray to get on.

Billy Ray stepped over the gap between the bucket and landing, grabbed hold of a vertical support, and clamped his eyes shut. He was sweating, and his knees felt weak. He was positive that if he loosened his hold on the steel upright even by a little he would topple out of the bucket and fall all the way to the bottom of the deep shaft. With his eyes tight shut and his face lifted he began to mouth a wordless prayer.

"Take 'er down, Danny," Artie said.

Billy Ray heard the familiar bell signal, heard the response from far below, and felt the bucket lurch sickeningly under his feet as the cage started a sharp, fast drop toward Four Level thousands of feet down.

Chapter 37

The dust was so thick that a man couldn't see, much less breathe. Even after Billy Ray got his lamp lighted, he could not really see. The light coming off the reflector hit the dust that was hanging in the air and diffused into it, making dim ghost shapes of anything or anyone more than a few feet away. Men materialized in front of him and then disappeared again, half-seen figures rushing back and forth with jagged chunks of rock to throw into the shaft or simply rushing back and forth. There was little order yet to the rescue effort.

"Alphabet. Damn you, Alphabet, where are you?" Billy Ray recognized the shift foreman's voice.

"Right beside you, pret' near," Artie said calmly. The stolid Bohunk had himself under control even if no one else seemed to.

"Get back on that bucket, Alphabet. I

want you to take some of these boys up and bring replacements down. We're gonna work like hell and have to change off often. Tell 'em up above that we need timbers. And a bellows to try and force air through the pile. You got that?"

"Timbers, bellows, lots of reliefs. I got that."

"Good. Bring the first relief down, then take a couple of them with you and go down to Five Level. I'll keep the boys from dumping any rock down on top of you while you do it. We need the ore carts from Five Level. All the damn carts from Four are behind the cave-in. They'll make the clearing go faster than trying to carry it by hand. While you're doing that I'll rig a stop at the landing here so we can run the carts up to it and dump from them right here. You got that?"

"I got."

"Bring the carts up from Five Level first, then go up and see if there are any sitting on Three or Two. I can't remember, but . . ."

"No carts on Two," a voice cut in. The speaker, whoever he was, was hidden in the curtain of hanging dust. "There are a couple left on Three."

"Okay," the foreman said. "Soon as you

get the carts off Five, go get the ones from Three and bring them down. We can muscle the empties off the tracks to make room for all of them once we get things sorted out."

"Gotcha," Artie said. A moment later Billy Ray heard the bell signal from the direction of the bucket, and Artie was gone.

With no ventilation deep in the shaft there was no air movement to speak of, and the dust continued to hang suspended in the air. Eventually it would settle out, but that would take even longer on the other side of the cave-in where there was no link with the outside world through the shaft. Breathing would be almost impossible back there.

There was no way to tell from here how far back it was to the cave-in. No way to judge from the sounds of men grunting and prying at the loose rock either. Sound seemed to travel with eerie effect through the dust, making it impossible to judge direction or distance either one.

Yellow glows moved here and there through the dust, marking the passage of boys wearing their lamps. Only rarely could he see who they were.

It soon became apparent that the boys were guiding on the rails laid on the stone floor to handle the ore carts. The men shuffled along with their shoes in contact with one rail, unable to see where they were going but able to feel and to follow the track that way, the right track leading into the tunnel and the left one coming back out. The boys were beginning to organize themselves while the foreman stayed back by the tunnel mouth and kept anybody from walking right on over the edge into the shaft.

Billy Ray pressed the side of his shoe against the right track and began to shuffle forward, following it toward the cave-in and the tons of rock that filled what was left of the tunnel.

Chapter 38

Billy Ray found a little niche gouged out of the wall and crawled into it. He leaned against the stone and trembled, from fatigue and cold alike.

There wasn't a part of his body that did not hurt. His hands were raw and oozing blood from the constant abrading of the rocks being pulled from the pile. His back and legs and arms ached from the constant lifting and carrying.

At least it was better now than it had been. The carts made things go quicker, but even so it was hard to tell if they were making any progress.

At least the air was not quite so bad now. There was still dust in the tunnel, but visibility had improved to twenty-five, thirty feet or so. It was possible now to recognize people. Or would have been if he had known any of them. Everybody he could see now was a stranger, boys in from the other mines but working just as hard as the Chagra stiffs did. Breaking their backs, practically working at a dead run to try and get through while there was still a chance for the Four Level bunch.

Now that he was no longer laboring and sweating Billy Ray was conscious of the cold. He did not know what the temperature was down at this level, but it was dang chilly. A damp, cutting chill too. He wished he had thought to snag a coat out of the changing room when he got the lamp, but he hadn't and now it was long too late.

He shivered some and groaned out loud. Someone — a man who looked and dressed like a boss but who was down here with the stiffs — heard him and came over to him. "Are you all right, son?"

"I'm fine," Billy Ray said wearily.

"The bucket will be bringing a new relief down soon. Why don't you ride it up when it goes?"

Billy Ray shook his head. He was just too dang tired to argue about it, but he could probably out-stubborn anybody on the mountain if it came down to it.

The man didn't have time or interest for arguing anyway. He turned away and hurried after another boss-looking fellow who was heading down the tunnel toward the cave-in.

Billy Ray felt inside his shirt and found the sweaty lump of dough that had been bread and the twist of paper that held the jam he had bought. That was supposed to have been his supper.

Still would do, he decided. There would be hot food being handed out at the bunkhouse for all the boys who'd come, but getting any of that would mean going up top again. He was afraid if he took the bucket up some of the Chagra bosses would recognize him and keep him from coming down again.

He pulled the twist of paper out and tore at the corner until the jam was exposed, then sucked on it. It was strawberry. It tasted sweet and good to him, and after he had sucked all of it out of the paper that he could he opened it up and licked it clean.

For hours — heck, for he didn't know how long — he had been trying to avoid thinking about it, but now that he had stopped for a moment he became aware all over again of how much rock there was between his head and the sky and sunshine above.

"Jesus," he whispered.

Even so he could feel a tightness in his

chest, like the weight of all that rock was lying on his ribs, pushing at him, and trying to crush him. It was difficult to breathe.

"Jesus," he said again.

He thought about his Bible. He had left it someplace and could not remember where. It had to be somewhere close, though. He had not left this end of the tunnel since he had come down, not except to haul rock to the shaft or once in a while to help push the carts back and forth once they had been brought up.

"Jesus."

Tommy was back on the other side of that pile somewhere. And Rick. And half a dozen other boys.

He could hear the hard clunk of rock hitting steel and thumping against more rock as the stone was pried out of the pile and thrown into the carts.

Men cussed softly as they worked and panted from the strain of it. There wasn't a one of them that was dogging it. Not down here. Not now.

Under that sound was the softer thunk and sigh of the bellows working, slow and steady and unrelenting as boys worked the handles up and down. Billy Ray thought it was the set of bellows from the forge that had been brought down. They had fixed a canvas hose to it off some pump somewhere and shoved that into the pile as far as they could, trying to force air back to the Four Level boys. Nobody had any idea if it was working or not, but they weren't going to quit trying because of that.

The carts rumbled slowly past, rolling down the tracks with goggle-eyed men straining to move them faster, rolling back almost at a run so they could be filled again. With all that tonnage being dumped into the bucket shaft the Chagra was going to have a heck of a time getting started again once this was over. No one cared about that right now.

"You got to get over on the other side of that pile and help them, Lord," Billy Ray whispered.

It was bad enough here. He could imagine all too well what it must be like over there.

He could feel the rock overhead pushing down on him again. There was no time to be thinking about that, though.

With a groan of protest slipping out past tight-clenched lips and jaw he forced himself back to his feet. His hands were hurting, but he could work the bellows and free one of those boys to pull rock. He stepped up to the thing and took hold of the handle, motioning the fellow who was working it to go on.

The man nodded and stepped away.

Billy Ray bent his back to the handles, listening to the sigh of rushing air as the leather envelope forced life-giving air down the hose. "Let it reach 'em, Lord. Let it reach them, please."

Chapter 39

The digging reached a side stope sometime . . . Billy Ray wasn't sure . . . maybe on the third day or the fourth. Time was not real clear for him by then. The one time he had gone up top . . . practically had been carried up top . . . it had been night. It seemed an awfully long time since he had last seen the sun. He had missed services, he knew that. Just hadn't shown up for it and had not even thought about it until he overheard a fellow say something about it being Monday. And that had been quite a while ago. He had no idea what day or night it was now. Reaching the stope would have been cause for rejoicing because then they had another place to dump rock from the pile except that right at the mouth of the stope they found a body.

Billy Ray had been picking rock close by when they found him. There weren't any other Chagra boys in the hole right then, so it had been up to Billy Ray to identify him and send the word up while the crew worked to uncover him enough that they could pull the body free and send it up.

It was Brian F., the boy who'd sworn he would never again work Four Level because the tommyknockers had warned him out of it.

He'd been afraid if he ever went back to Four he would die there. Billy Ray shuddered, remembering Brian talking about the tommyknockers, swearing he would not be part of the Four Level crew. He'd been here, tommyknockers or no, and now he was dead, lying there all mussed and gray under the rock on Four Level.

Billy Ray said a prayer over Brian while a bunch of boys from the Tophat pulled him out from under the rock and carried him to the cage to be taken up top.

Before that bunch had gotten a dozen feet away the rest of the crew was busy again, pulling rock off the pile and flinging it into the open stope where Brian had died.

Billy Ray shivered, from the cold and maybe from something more, and went back to work. He was past the point of being tired now. He was light-headed and feeling fuzzy all over, but he could still work. That was what counted. He could still work.

Chapter 40

It was Friday morning that they called all the boys down from the hoist shed and out of the bunkhouse and from practically every patch of level ground anywhere around the Chagra No. 1, called in all of them who were not underground at the moment. There were an awful lot of them, from every mine in the gorge and some even in from neighboring towns half a mountain range away.

They called them together on the south side of the mill building and Mr. Valdura and the rest of the Chagra bosses stood in the door where the crusher operator threw out the cull rock and the ore chunks that were too big to go through the stamp.

At first there was a buzz of expectation that ran through the crowd, everybody thinking there must be good news from down below because why else would all the bosses be there.

Then they got a look at the expressions on those bosses, and the murmuring changed from excitement to anger.

"We want you all to know how much we, all of us, appreciate the help you have given. That will not be forgotten by any man on this mountain. But we have been in consultation with our own engineers and with every engineer and geologist we can reach. Our belief is that it would serve no purpose to carry on, men. We have reached the reluctant conclusion that the time has come to seal off Four Level and mark it as the permanent resting place of seven good men and true."

The boys who had gathered hoping to hear good news turned their eyes toward the ground. Not one of them seemed to want to look at any other.

Billy Ray had been lying on the dump below the mill, too exhausted to move.

He came to his feet, shaking his head. Shaking his fist now up toward Valdura and the rest of the bosses. They cared. They, all of them, had done their best. He knew that. He was angry anyway.

"No!" he shouted. His voice was loud and carried for all of them to hear.

"No," he roared again. He shook his head. His thoughts were foggy and unclear, but he felt the need to speak too strongly to ignore it.

"Back in Matthew. When I was readin' in Matthew . . ."

Men around him were beginning to mutter. "What the hell is this?" he heard someone ask in a complaining tone.

Billy Ray took a deep breath and started over. "I remember when I was reading in Matthew," he said in a loud, clear voice. "The Lord says in Matthew that if we have a grain of faith no bigger'n a mustard seed, why, we can move whole mountains. With just that speck of faith, we could move this whole mountain. With just that speck of faith we can dang sure clear out one tunnel."

"But those men are . . ."

"They are *not* dead. They aren't. They're in there and they're still alive. I have faith that they're alive. I have faith that's bigger'n some dang seed of mustard." He turned and stared around him in a circle, then back up toward Valdura and the Chagra bosses. "Have you ever seen a mustard seed? I have. I've ground a many of them up for Doc Hoosier for people wanting to make mustard plasters. I can tell you that a mustard seed ain't very dang big. And no more faith than that is what it takes. Well, dang it, I got that faith. I'm telling you that those boys are still alive in there. They're down below our feet this very minute waiting for us to come and fetch them. I promise you that. The Lord God promises you that. And I say we don't stop until we get to them."

"You dumb . . ."

"Hold it." The man who cut in was big and dust filthy and looked as tired as Billy Ray felt.

"All of you hold it," Valdura shouted. "Halstad, I know you probably believe that, but . . ."

"Dammit, I said to hold it an' I mean you too," the big man said. He glared up at Valdura and then at the men around him. "I don't know about any of this mustard seed shit, but I can tell you this. There isn't a son of a bitch on this mountain has worked harder or done more down in that hole than the sky pilot here. And I'm with him, by God. Beggin' your pardon, rev'rend. I didn't mean that like it sounded."

Billy Ray nodded.

"If this preacher-man says those boys are still alive an' is willing to back it up that strong, well, dammit, I say we dig. We dig till we get live men or dead bodies out of there. The hell with a seal an' a plaque. We dig till those boys are outa the damn ground. And if they come out alive, by God, then I'm goin' to the rev'rend's services Sunday morning an' I'll expect to see every livin' one of you sons of bitches there with me."

The man put his hands on his hips and sent a challenging stare up toward Valdura and the Chagra bosses.

"Well?" he demanded.

Valdura looked around to see what the others thought, but none of them were meeting his eyes. He looked back down toward Billy Ray and toward the big miner who had supported him. "All right," he said softly.

A cheer went up from the boys, and they began to surge toward the Chagra, ready to have another go at it underground.

Chapter 41

It was Sunday evening when they broke through to the far end of the blockage. Billy Ray was down in the hole, working the bellows along with a weak-lunged Welshman from the Bigelow mine, when the shout went up.

All through the tunnel men dropped what they were doing and peered down toward the cave-in pile.

"Keep the air coming, dammit. We got the hose through, and they're clearing the way now," someone called. Billy Ray and the little Welshman started the bellows working again.

The word seemed impossibly long in coming. Billy Ray was trembling, as much from anticipation as from fatigue.

Then he laughed at himself and relaxed. If he'd had faith enough before he might as well keep it now.

The word came finally down the long, dim tunnel, passed along with grins and backslapping and yelps of exuberation that no amount of tiredness could dampen.

"They're alive, by God. They're in lousy shape, but they're alive back there."

Men who were trying to crowd forward inside the confinement of the tunnel walls made way as Billy Ray left the bellows and ran toward the Four Level boys.

The hole that had been cleared was little better than a rat hole, and the ceiling was unshored, but no one seemed to care about that at the moment. Billy Ray didn't either.

Men lay on their backs along the length of the narrow passage and passed the rescued men hand over hand to pull them out beyond the blockage.

More hands pulled them free as soon as they reached open tunnel.

Billy Ray saw Tommy being lifted clear. He moved forward and tried to help carry him, but all of a sudden he was too weary to manage it. He went down, his knees buckling and no longer able to support him.

Other men had to carry the rescued boys out through the long tunnel.

Someone helped Billy Ray to his feet. Someone else found his Bible and pushed it into his hands.

For some reason the boys down below were slapping him on the back and congratulating him like he had done this all by himself.

Which he knew damn good and well he hadn't.

And it hadn't just been these boys down in the hole who had done it either.

He was going to have something to talk about for the next services. That was for sure.

Grinning and crying and weaving from side to side on rubbery legs, Billy Ray followed the crowd out toward the bucket. He wasn't the only one crying, either.

The first lift was already gone by the time he reached the shaft, already carrying three of the rescued boys and all of the good word up toward the top. Tommy was lying near the edge, mostly out of his mind with delirium but conscious enough to suck on a water bottle someone was holding for him. All of them would have been having to lick seepage off the floor to get any water for the past eight days. That would have been worse than being without food.

But there would be time enough to hear about their end of it later.

Billy Ray slumped down onto the floor

and got on his knees. He looked up, way beyond the rock ceiling that was overhead and far past the mountain they were inside.

"Thanks," he whispered.

Chapter 42

Billy Ray slept like a lump through Sunday night, dozed Monday away, and slept hard again Monday night. He felt almost halfway close to human when he woke Tuesday morning, although he probably smelled like a mule. Doc Hoosier had put salve on his hands and rubbed liniment into his back and shoulders and arms every time he woke up on Monday. Still, Doc's medications seemed to have done some good. He could move without hollering in pain nearly every time he tried it now.

Doc must have heard him moving around Tuesday morning because he came into the back room about the time Billy Ray was getting dressed.

"Do you feel up to coming out to the shop now?" he asked.

"Sure, Doc. And I'm sure sorry about taking so much time off. What d'you need?"

Hoosier gave him an odd look and went with him out into the shop. There were a bunch of men there, but they had not come as customers. There was Fischer from the Chagra and a couple of the supervisors and some of the boys too.

"These gentlemen wanted to see you," Doc said.

Billy Ray waited for them to speak their piece.

It was Fischer who was talking for them. "We, uh, that is, Reverend Halstad, we were hoping you would be willing to hold the burial services for Brian Fartle. If that would be convenient, that is."

"Of course I could do that."

"This afternoon?"

Billy Ray nodded.

"Fine. We, uh, will assemble at the upper end of town around one. If that is acceptable to you, Reverend Halstad."

Reverend. Good grief, even Fischer was doing it now. But all Billy Ray said was, "Whenever you say, sir."

"Thank you. Thank you very much." Fischer actually looked relieved. That was fairly mystifying, but Billy Ray was not going to worry about it. "One o'clock, then."

"Yes, sir. I'll be there."

Billy Ray spent the rest of the morning helping Doc get his stock back in shape. It was difficult trying to hold the pestle with his hands still so raw, but a little salve and the use of gloves helped. He felt bad enough about laying off so much lately. If he up and got fired from this job now he would feel even worse about it, so he made it a point to not shirk.

"I never thought to ask, Doc, if it would be all right for me to go an' speak for Brian."

Doc gave him another funny look but told him to go ahead.

Come one o'clock Billy Ray got a heck of a surprise. The funeral procession for Brian F. was a full turnout. It looked like every man from every mine in the gorge was down for it and most of the town people too.

They had the casket loaded onto one big wagon, and there was another one trailing it with chairs set inside so the boys who'd been rescued from Four Level could ride behind the coffin wagon. The wagon with Brian's coffin in it was draped with black cloth, and from someplace they had put together a funeral band of sorts with horns and drums and some fifes. Billy Ray recognized several of the musicians as coming from the saloons but most of them he did not know.

Fischer greeted him like the man had not expected him to really come even though Billy Ray had said he would. "You can ride with the, uh, survivors, Reverend Halstad."

Billy Ray took a look around him. Most of the boys close by were fellows he hadn't known before but now could recognize from the rescue effort. "Naw," he said. "Most of these fellows have done a lot more'n me lately, and they're wore out too. I reckon I'll walk, but I thank you."

That was just fine with Fischer. Billy Ray got the impression that about anything he said or wanted would be just fine with Fischer today.

The procession got under way not more than twenty minutes late, which was not bad. The band led the way, then the coffin wagon, then the wagon with Tommy and Rick and the other rescued boys in it, then the Chagra bosses and some bosses from other mines, then Billy Ray and the rest of the boys down from the mines.

Not quite everybody in town went along, of course. Most did, though, and all along the street until they got clear of the town buildings there were whores leaning out the windows and waving black garters or lace things or whatever. They were making a show out of mourning, but Billy Ray figured they were really more interested in drumming up business and keeping the working boys from being mad at them than in really caring about one stiff going and dying.

The procession marched slow up the creek, toward the cemetery there, and across the bridge that led over toward the Tophat and some of the smaller mines. The bridge washed out during the spring melt every year, and the outfits on that side rebuilt it every year.

Somebody had already been up and dug the grave, and there were chairs near it for the survivors to sit on and more chairs for the bosses. After the coffin was unloaded and put near the open grave it took quite a while for the crowd to all get there. They just came and kept on coming. Billy Ray hadn't had any idea there were so many people in the gorge, but getting nearly all of them here in one spot was a real eye-opener. There were ten times as many people as he'd ever imagined seeing in one place at one time.

While they were waiting for them to all

get as close as they could, Fischer sidled over beside him.

"There is, uh, a great favor we would like to ask you, Reverend Halstad. Not just the Chagra Corporation but all of the companies operating here."

"Me? A favor? Whatever about?"

"Yes, well, there have been rumors, you see."

"Rumors?" Billy Ray was beginning to feel like a dang parrot, but he couldn't help it.

"Rumors. You know. About a memorial service? I mean, we all understand that the men are entitled to attend the funeral for this, uh, Brian. But there has been talk that you intend to hold a special service tomorrow, Reverend Halstad."

Billy Ray shook his head. "That's the first I've heard anything about it, Mr. Fischer."

"Are you sure about that?"

"I am not lying to you, Mr. Fischer."

"No. Of course not. I never meant to imply any such thing. But surely you understand. I mean, if you were to call a special service in the middle of the week, after that stunt you pulled last week, why, you would shut the entire mountain down. And we have missed quite enough production already because of this. To say nothing of the pay the men would forfeit. You do understand that, I am sure."

"Shut down? Look, Mr. Fischer, obviously you know more about this than me. But I couldn't shut anything down. Wouldn't if I could anyhow. And as for you calling that rescue a stunt, well, sir, I can't say as I like that. What the Good Lord decides to do ain't any stunt, sir. Not no way."

"No. Please. I didn't mean to call it a, uh, a stunt. A slip of the tongue, Reverend Halstad. You say you do not intend any midweek service?"

"Of course not. Good grief, man."

"You, uh, do understand our concern, I'm sure."

"No, dang it, I don't. Sounds to me like you think I'm gonna do something to hurt the companies or the boys or worse. You people just haven't figured out yet, I guess, that I'm not here to hurt nothing or nobody. I'm trying to pass along the gift of salvation that was given to me. Nothing more than that. Now can we get on with this?"

"Yes, of course. Please do, Reverend Halstad."

Billy Ray shook his head some and took

his place in front of the grave. The cemetery was laid out on a hillside so he could see out over the heads of the crowd that had come. He still couldn't hardly believe there were so many of them, but of course they had all come out to pay their respects to Brian and probably even more to share their good feeling with Tommy and Rick and the other boys who'd made it.

He looked them over and then he began to talk. He told them some about Brian. He told them more about the Lord, as this was the best chance he would ever have to reach most of these boys. He thanked the fellows who'd pitched in to help, on behalf of the boys who'd made it and for Brian who they'd tried to help and for the Lord who had really been behind it all. He remembered to thank the companies because they had done their part too. Then finally he stepped off to the side and helpers representing each of the mines came up to lower the coffin into the ground and then to fill the grave after Billy Ray dropped the first handful of dirt in. The seven survivors were the honorary pallbearers, but none of them was strong enough to actually do anything except to pitch a handful of dirt in. Then the whole thing was over, and the crowd broke up and started drifting back downhill. There would be some serious drinking and fornicating going on tonight as the boys celebrated being alive now that Brian was in the ground.

"Can we offer you a ride, Reverend Halstad?"

Billy Ray shook his head, and the wagons rolled off, Rick turning to yell back that he would see Billy Ray Sunday morning if not before and some of the other survivors, even Tommy, looking at him funny.

Billy Ray was still feeling puny, and the walk up had not done anything to take the kinks out of his muscles. He headed back slowly, trailing behind everybody else.

By the time he reached the rowdy end of the town things were popping there, loud and raucous, with the curtains drawn over the windows where the whores had been showing themselves a little while earlier and the sounds of merriment and the smell of beer coming out of all the open saloon doors.

Billy Ray was almost back to Doc Hoosier's shop, looking forward to getting acquainted with his cot again as quickly as possible, when Murphy stepped out in front of him.

"You son of a bitch," the little man

hissed at him. "You had to go and side with management, didn't you."

Before Billy Ray had time to say anything — or to think of anything to say if he had had any time — Murphy was gone, scurrying off up the street in a hightail hurry.

Billy Ray looked after the idiot and had to conclude that Murphy was as weird in his way as Fischer was in his. Fortunately Billy Ray didn't have to worry about either of them.

Chapter 43

Billy Ray got up extra early Wednesday to get the shop swept out and the grinding done. He'd done everything he knew to do plus had the shelves straightened and re-stocked before Doc Hoosier ever came downstairs to say good morning.

"What put the bee in your bonnet so early?" Doc asked.

"Well, sir, I was kinda hoping . . ."

"That girl you've been seeing?"

"Yes, sir," Billy Ray hadn't realized that Doc knew about Miss Hattie, but he certainly was not going to lie about it.

"All right, then. I don't need you back here until lunchtime. Then I'd like you to take over while I get something to eat. Fair enough?"

"Yes, sir. More than." With a grin Billy Ray rolled his sleeves down and headed for the door.

He stopped in at Mercheson's and

bought two crullers to take down to the creek with him. He would have liked to be able to take more and make a regular picnic out of it, but he was having to watch his pennies. Not that he needed so very much, but that stint down in the mine had ruined his everyday clothes. He was going to have to replace all of it, right down to the shoes. And likely someone would be taking up a collection to help the seven Four Level boys along until they could get back to work. He wanted to be able to kick in for that. Anyway, one cruller to eat and another to share, that would do. The important thing would be to see Miss Hattie again after so long.

This morning he didn't stop to visit with Mercheson. He took his crullers, wrapped in paper, and set off down the road at a pace that was as close to being a run as he could comfortably manage. He was still pretty sore but was feeling rested now.

He hurried through town and down to the turnoff he had come to know so well, then did break into a run as he approached the top of the creek bank.

He came to a halt there, though, and stood looking up and down the rocky creek bed.

Hattie wasn't there, darn it. And after so

long he'd really been looking forward to seeing her again.

He picked his way slowly down the steep side of the bank to level territory and found a seat on a rock. It was still early. She might come yet.

He waited until it was nearly time to head back to the shop before he ate his cruller. Waited until the last minute and ate the second one while he was walking back up the road to town. It was a funny thing, but he was feeling those aches and pains again now after forgetting them for a while there.

That evening after work he hiked up to the Chagra and visited with the boys there. They, all of them, even Tommy, seemed glad to see him, and there was a lot of rehashing of the ordeal so it was late before he got home that night.

Next morning he was up early again, though, heading for the creek with two crullers wrapped in paper. But again there was no sign of Miss Hattie. Not that morning nor any other the whole rest of the week, right up until Sunday.

It was distressing, of course, but there was no reason . . . actually . . . why she mightn't have moved on without saying anything to him or leaving a message.

Then too, heck, she could have tried to find him to say goodbye but not been able to while he was up at the mine during the troubles.

It bothered him, but he would get over it. It wasn't like there'd been anything said between them. Not really. He didn't say anything to Doc about it, of course, and made it a point to work extra hard for the man to make up for all the time Billy Ray had been away lately.

Saturday night he sat down with his battered, old, pages-missing Bible and worked up what he thought should be a pretty good talk for services tomorrow. It was built all on faith and works and how the one could lead to the other. He would have been willing to bet that tomorrow morning he would have fifty folks to talk to. Maybe even more than that.

Chapter 44

Good Lord! Fifty folks? There were *hundreds* of them.

Billy Ray was walking up the road from the creek, where he'd gone early hoping to find Miss Hattie, and he guessed he surprised the crowd coming from that direction about as bad as they did him by so many of them being there.

He'd started marveling at there being so many of them as soon as he came into sight and kept it up the whole way to where the choir was gathered. The ladies in the choir looked flustered, and Harry Small looked to be so nervous Billy Ray was expecting him to drop his concertina in the middle of the first hymn.

There were people — stiffs, mostly, still in their Saturday night clothes and some of them several sheets to the wind yet — purely filling up the open lot they'd been using for services. They were backed up all the way to the edge of town and up the hillside until it got too steep to stand on and right smack across the roadway to the creek bank.

Good Lord. He couldn't begin to count how many of them there might be. It was packed so full that his regular folks were about lost in the crowd. Billy Ray could see some of them, the ladies' hats sticking up here and there among the sea of bleary, bearded faces. And he spotted Tommy Johnson near the front. He couldn't see Rick, but he had to be somewhere close. Likely he was the one who had talked Tommy into coming.

Billy Ray grinned and stood on his tiptoes to see all of them there.

Someone out front spotted him finally, and a cheer went up.

Billy Ray couldn't hardly believe that. Certainly he didn't know what it was for.

The boys kept up their hoorahing until he waved his hands and finally quieted them down. "What the heck is all the cheering about?"

"After what you done last week you want to ask that?" someone returned.

"Me? Huh uh, boys. All I done last week was the same as you. Less than a lot o' you." He grinned at them. "But I sure know where the credit does belong, boys, and that's what I come to talk to you about."

There was some more whooping and hollering. Those boys were wrong, of course, but the plain fact was that they made Billy Ray feel pretty good. That was wrong, probably, taking pride for something he hadn't done. But he couldn't help it.

He got them quiet again and raised his voice so he could be heard at the back. "We got a real treat for you boys today. We got some ladies up here who can sing a hymn that'd make a nightingale cry for jealousy, and then I got some things to say that I reckon you all got to hear. Because the Lord, He c'n do for you what He's already done for me. And that's a lot, boys. I'm here to tell you that that's a lot."

Billy Ray was ready to step back and turn it over to the choir, but there was a commotion coming up through the middle of the crowd. It took him a minute to get a look at what was causing it.

Then he could see a small knot of hard-faced toughs forcing their way through, pushing and shoving and not being any too gentle about it either. One of them gave Mrs. Horvath a shove — probably by accident — and she whacked him with her handbag but then got out of their way right smart.

Billy Ray got his first inkling of what was up when he spotted that dang Lem Murphy with them.

Murphy's bullyboys got the little idiot up close and then stood all in a tight bunch in front of everybody while Murphy came right up beside Billy Ray and turned to face all the boys.

Everybody was curious, Billy Ray included, and there was a hush while people waited to see what was what.

Murphy wasn't tall enough to see over the crowd like Billy Ray could, so he took a folding chair that belonged to one of the ladies who was standing up front ready to sing with the choir. Murphy stood on that so folks could see and hear him.

"Before you boys start taking this sell-out son of a bitch's word for gospel you'd better listen to what kind of lying preacher you have here."

Billy Ray didn't know what Murphy meant by that bull, but he wasn't going to have his service broken up. He took a step forward and would have yanked Murphy down off the chair, but a couple of Murphy's boys grabbed his arms and held him more or less still.

"Now it's one thing for this liar to side with management," Murphy was saying. "Like we all heard him do last Tuesday at that poor dead boy's burying. I can't say anything about that. But I want you to know what kind of man you've been listening to."

Murphy motioned with his hand — there was no point in him trying to say anything for the moment because there was some growling going on in the crowd — and the rest of his boys pressed forward in their tight little formation.

Murphy waved for silence and after a bit got it. "You heard me right," he shouted. "This so-called preacher, who isn't a preacher at all to begin with, tells you boys about salvation. He tells you not to sin. But what kind of man is he? I'll show you what kind of preacher he is. He's the kind of lying SOB of a preacher that consorts with whores. And I say we don't listen to his kind. If you want help, me and Bill Haywood can give it to you. But not some make-believe preacher that consorts with whores."

Billy Ray thought the man had lost his mind, what little he'd had to begin with.

Then the bunch of Murphy's men came forward and lifted up from their midst a

278

crying, cringing Miss Hattie Markle to be put on public display in front of all those people.

Hattie was dressed in a skimpy, short-length skirt and had red rouge smeared over her cheeks and lips. She looked the part of a whore, all right, and there was a change in the tone of the growling that was going through the crowd now.

"This is the kind of woman your lyin' preacher runs with all during the week. And Sundays too." Lem Murphy stood there looking damned smug.

Chapter 45

Hattie was huddled in against herself like she wished she could make herself small, but she couldn't. Everybody who could see was staring at her, and those that couldn't were trying. She was red in the face from shame until the rouge was hardly noticeable.

Lem Murphy pointed to her but said nothing more. He didn't have to. There was a rumble of muttering from the crowd.

The first to shout out was Mrs. Harmon, who Billy Ray remembered thought highly of her own righteousness. She stamped toward the front of the crowd and gave Hattie and then Billy Ray a glare, then she yelled something about harlots and whoremasters, and some other folks took that up. Including, Billy Ray noticed, those two friends of Murphy's who had been coming to the services right along.

Murphy jumped down off his chair and folded his arms. He gave Billy Ray a tight, satisfied little smile and said, "Now try and get them with you, you son of a bitch."

Billy Ray smiled at the little fool and jumped up onto the chair.

The folks saw him and quieted down real quick. Likely they were expecting denials they could hoot at or whimpering that would give them a laugh.

Shee-oot, Billy Ray thought. If he didn't have any better on his side of the fence than Lemuel Murphy and his tricks, why, he would deserve to get run out of Blue Gorge and not stop until he got to the neighborhood of those tall clipper ships.

Billy Ray took his time before he spoke, standing there looking from one pair of eyes to another and finally coming to rest right on that Mrs. Harmon's, who was looking as puffed up as a setting hen and twice as pouty.

He reached down and held his hand for Miss Hattie to hold onto. She looked like she needed some comforting and support in the middle of all that bunch now. He smiled at her and winked. She tried to smile back but couldn't manage quite that much. Her face was tear-streaked and messy, and she looked a sight. "Don't you fret," Billy Ray said to her in a soft voice.

Then he looked up toward the crowd

and spoke louder so that everyone could hear.

"This girl is Miss Hattie Markle." He paused. "I have picnicked with Miss Hattie along the creek down below here. I have talked with her. I have even had hopes that she would find me to be a favorable sort of fellow. That I have done." He nodded and looked across the mass of heads, again though coming back to look Mrs. Harmon square in the eyes.

"This isn't what I come here to talk about this morning. But we'll get to that in a bit. Right now I want you boys . . . you ladies too . . . to listen close to something I read a while back. John, I think it was, but I could be wrong about that."

He took his time. He was in no hurry. Felt no worries either. However the Good Lord wanted to roll this, Billy Ray was willing to roll with it.

"Some of you may've heard this story before. Maybe not. It happened when Jesus was doing some teaching, had a crowd of folks gathered around to listen to whatever His subject was that day. The Bible don't say, so I can't tell you about that. But I can tell you what happened while He was trying to preach to those folks.

"Along came this bunch of big shots. I

282

forget what they were called, but that's what they were. A bunch of big shots who wanted to trap the Lord in something wrong so they could claim He was a liar."

That shot found a mark with some of them. A lot of eyes went from Billy Ray or Miss Hattie toward Murphy, who was still standing there looking smug.

"Those big shots were dragging along behind them this poor little ol' gal who'd been caught doing what she shouldn't. Caught right in the act, they said. And they dared Jesus t' do something about it. Y'know why? Because the law back then was that anybody caught like that girl had been was supposed to be killed. Everybody was supposed to stand back and throw rocks at her until she was dead. That was the law, and those big shots knew it and they were daring Jesus to have a say-so about that poor, scared girl. Because if Jesus said they was to stone her to death, why, then this love and salvation stuff He'd been teaching would pretty much have to be a bunch of hogwash. But if Jesus said they was to let that girl go, why, He'd be telling them to break the law and commit that kind of sin. So those big shots figured they had Jesus where they wanted Him so that He couldn't wiggle off the hook nohow."

Mrs. Harmon was beginning to look a tad uncomfortable, like she'd have been happier if Billy Ray would look someplace other than at her.

"Had Jesus on the hook, those boys figured. But d'you know what He did? He told them to go right on an' enforce the law. But He went and added that the only folks who oughta be able to judge somebody that way was them as were free from sins themselves.

"Let him who's without sin throw that first stone. That's what Jesus told them. And there wasn't a one of them there that wasn't a sinner. There wasn't anybody in that whole big crowd that didn't need the forgiveness and the salvation that Jesus was offerin'."

Billy Ray let Mrs. Harmon relax for a bit. He looked at somebody else.

"Think about that," he said. "There wasn't anybody in that whole big crowd that was qualified to pick up a rock and chunk it at that girl. Because every one of them was a sinner his or her own self and needed forgiveness and needed salvation."

Billy Ray stood taller on top of the chair and pointed a finger down at Miss Hattie. "This girl here is a sinner. I am a sinner. If I had to make it to Heaven for being spotless, boys, I wouldn't have a chance. Neither would this girl here. Neither would you. You want to chunk rocks at her? Have at it, boys, ladies. But only if you're qualified for the job."

Billy Ray waited a bit, looking at them. Then he pointed down toward the ground. "There's rocks aplenty here. For anybody that wants to use one. D'you, Rick? You, Tommy? You, Daniel?" There wasn't anybody meeting his eyes now.

"We are all sinners," he shouted. "Every last one of us. But there isn't any one of us including this girl right here who's ever done anything that the Lord don't know about. Or that the Lord isn't willing to forgive.

"All any of us got to do to get that forgiveness is to ask for it.

"All you got to do to have every last one of your sins wiped clean and forgotten and a whole fresh slate given you to write on is to ask. All you got to do is tell the Lord you're sorry an' you want to be saved." His voice slowed and softened. "That's all, boys, ladies. Do that and this girl right here can be cleansed white as snow. She can be. Or you can be. Or you."

He lifted a finger and pointed it first at one stiff and then another, working around the circle of them that were facing him. Ending finally with his finger pointed down at Miss Hattie.

She began to cry and dropped to her knees, praying out loud for salvation in a voice that carried through the crowd.

Billy Ray got down off the chair and scooped Miss Hattie into his arms. "This newly saved girl needs baptizing," he said. "So unless somebody has something to say about that, I'm fixing to go tend to it. Anybody want to object?"

There was no answer.

Billy Ray looked around to see if Mr. Lemuel Murphy wanted to put a word in, but Murphy wasn't standing there anymore. The little creep had crept off someplace. His boys were standing around looking confused. Judging from some of the looks Billy Ray saw going in their direction, he didn't blame them for keeping their mouths shut with their boss gone.

"All right, then. And anybody else that feels the need for baptizing, you come right along. There's room in Heaven for everybody as wants to go there."

The middle of that creek got pretty crowded that morning, and Billy Ray Halstad shouted and grinned over each and every one of those who came to be baptized.

Chapter 46

Billy Ray looked up from the mortar where he was grinding some sulfur to be mixed with molasses. There were a bunch of people coming into the shop. A dozen of them, he guessed, and every one of them a long familiar face. They were mostly ladies. All of them except for Mrs. Harmon were from the faithful old congregation group that had been listening to him from the very beginning.

He would have been pleased to see them except for Mrs. Harmon being among them.

Still and all, if the Lord wanted Billy Ray to move along somewhere else, that was what he'd do. It certainly wouldn't be like he was leaving any great prospects behind.

For a change Harry Small took the lead and his wife hung toward the back. Likely this was the sort of thing that they would think a man should handle instead of the ladies.

Billy Ray laid his pestle down and stood. Doc must have guessed what was up, because he disappeared into the back, leaving Billy Ray alone with the folks.

"I've embarrassed all of you," Billy Ray said, "and I apologize for that. I don't apologize for what I did, mind. That I'd do all over again. But I am sorry for the trouble it put all of you through."

"What the devil are you talking about, Reverend?" Small asked.

"About last Sunday, of course. But you needn't worry. I can be gone from here before next Sunday comes around. If you like, if you'd trust me to do it, I can ask around in other places and see can I get a real preacher to come here."

Harry Small snorted, but it was Mrs. Harmon who stepped forward. Billy Ray remembered that she was a sniffer, not a snorter. Not that it mattered.

"You don't understand, Reverend Halstad. We don't want you to leave. We came to talk to you about building a church in Blue Gorge."

"And buying some hymnals," Mrs. Small put in.

"We couldn't pay you much," Harry added prudently.

"Maybe you folks don't understand

288

then," Billy Ray said. "This is more'n I ever expected. But you got to know, right up front. If I stay here in Blue Gorge an' take on the church, I'll go right on seeing Miss Markle. She won't be doing any of that kind of work anymore, and I would expect to call on her again just as soon as she can find a job and get located. If she stays here, that is. She might not, but I'll sure ask her to if I'm staying."

The rest of them turned to Mrs. Harmon for an answer. Mrs. Harmon didn't look like she liked it, particularly. She looked at Billy Ray for the longest time without saying anything. Then her eyes dropped away and she nodded.

"I'm glad you agree," Billy Ray said, "because clean is clean, just like saved is saved. An' the Lord don't just forgive, He forgets too."

"You ask a lot, Reverend Halstad."

"No, ma'am. It's not me doing the asking."

Mrs. Harmon sighed.

But she didn't sniff. Billy Ray thought that was an awfully good sign.

"You're sure?" he asked.

"We are," Small answered. The man smiled. "Couldn't find a better reverend anywhere this side of St. Louis, the way I see it. Maybe not there neither."

"All right, then," Billy Ray said. He was upright and serious with them, went around and shook hands with them each and every one, the ladies included.

When they were done he went with them to the door and gave them a solemn farewell. He closed the door behind them and stood at the front window watching silently until the congregation was well down the street.

When he turned back inside the shop there was a broad, silly grin spread across his face. He looked at Doc, who was just now coming out of the back room with a worried look on him. The Reverend Billy Ray Halstad gave Hoosier a happy wink and leaped high into the air.

"Waaa-*hoooo!*"

About the Author

Frank Roderus is the author of fourteen previous Double D Westerns, including *Stillwater Smith*, *Finding Nevada*, and *Leaving Kansas*, which won the Western Writers of America's Spur Award for Best Western Novel of 1983. He lives in Florida.